THE BOBBSEY TWINS
IN TULIP LAND

THE BOBBSEY TWINS BOOKS
By Laura Lee Hope

———————

"Oh!" cried Nan. "The calves are ruining all the beautiful tulips!"

The Bobbsey Twins in Tulip Land

The Bobbsey Twins
in Tulip Land

By

LAURA LEE HOPE

GROSSET & DUNLAP

Publishers   *New York*

The Bobbsey Twins in Tulip Land

CONTENTS

THE BOBBSEY TWINS
IN TULIP LAND

CHAPTER I

THE CONTRARY WINDMILL

"OH DEAR, Susie's lost her back and can't
stand up!" Flossie exclaimed.

"How could a paper doll lose her back when
she only has a front?" asked Freddie.

Flossie and Freddie, the younger twins of the
Bobbsey family, were playing in the grass in their
back yard. Flossie had brought a cardboard dollhouse outside, and a box of her favorite paper
dolls.

Freddie had consented to play with them for a
few minutes, although he wished he could think
of something better to do.

He had his wish when a lumber truck pulled
into the driveway. On the seat was smiling, good-
natured Sam, who worked for the twins' father.
He leaned out and called:

"I'se got a surprise fo' yo', Freddie. Come
here an' help me lift it out."

Freddie Bobbsey sprang to his feet and raced

to the truck. When it stopped, he climbed up on the back.

"It's a windmill!" he cried. "A real windmill! Oh, thank you, Sam!"

The kindly, white-haired Negro laughed. He said the windmill was only a toy, even though it was fairly large.

"When de wings go round an' round," he explained, "de windmill gwine pump water."

Freddie was very much excited and could hardly wait to try out his new toy. It was rather heavy—too heavy for Freddie to lift out by himself.

"Oh, that's be-yootiful!" cried Flossie, as Sam set down the new toy in the center of the yard. "Please make it go, Sam."

Sam spun the sails of the windmill, but they stopped a moment later.

"Too bad dere's no wind now," Sam commented. He looked up at the sky. "I think maybe if yo' wait a little while, Freddie, a breeze gwine come in."

He went on into the kitchen, leaving the twins to play with the windmill by themselves.

"I know what," said Freddie. "I'll blow on it. You help me, Flossie."

Freddie blew and blew until he was red in the face. Flossie blew until she started to cough. The wings of the windmill had not moved more than an inch.

"Let's get a fan," Flossie suggested, and ran into the house.

She knew where there was a big, old-fashioned palm-leaf fan that no one ever used. The little girl seemed to remember hearing that it had belonged to her mother's grandmother.

Flossie tugged and tugged at the bureau drawer in which the fan was kept. Finally she got the drawer open, took out the big palm leaf, and hurried downstairs.

The twins took turns waving the fan as hard as they could. The wings of the windmill moved a little bit, but would not go far. Finally, Freddie gave an enormous sigh and flopped down on the grass.

"This old windmill gives me a pain," he said.

"You'd better not let Sam hear you say that," Flossie advised her twin. "He prob'ly spent a lot of money to buy it."

Freddie scowled. "If he did, the man he bought it from ought to take it back and give him a new one. I'm going to tell him."

Without stopping to think, the little boy hurried into the kitchen and told the colored man what was on his mind. Sam smiled.

"I'se sorry de windmill won't work," he said.

"I guess it's 'cause it's been played with too much. It's not a new windmill."

He explained that while he had been delivering lumber for Mr. Bobbsey, a woman had asked him if he knew anyone who would like the old windmill. She had no further use for it. Sam immediately had thought of Freddie, and believed the little boy would like to have it.

"Tonight, after I git home from de lumberyard, I'll fix de windmill fo' yo'," Sam promised.

Freddie was satisfied, and went back to playing paper dolls with Flossie. He offered to put a new back on Susie, and spent nearly half an hour up in his room, cutting pieces of cardboard, and trying to get the right shape to make the paper doll stand up.

When he had accomplished this, Freddie got a pot of glue and finished the job. He finally came out and presented Susie to his twin. The little girl opened her eyes very wide.

"Freddie, look at yourself!" she exclaimed. "Susie's all glued together, but so are you!"

Freddie looked at the sweater he was wearing. Instead of lying smoothly across his chest, it had humps and bumps in it where the glue had run down the front and dried. The little boy's hair was standing every which way, too. Some of it, stiff with glue, stuck straight out from his head.

"You'd better go wash the glue off," Flossie advised. She grinned. "If you don't, Mother or Dinah will do it."

Freddie made a face. If there was one thing he did not like, it was to have his mother or Dinah wash his hair. Dinah, who was Sam's wife, cooked for the Bobbsey family.

Suddenly the little boy's expression changed. He looked at the glue on his sweater, then at the windmill, and finally turned around completely and looked toward the garage. Flossie knew something was up.

"What are you going to do?" she asked.

Freddie's answer was most unexpected. "I'm going to get the hose, and make the wings on the windmill turn around," he said.

Flossie was not sure her twin should use the hose without permission, but she was so curious to see what was going to happen that she said nothing. The little girl did think of her paper dolls, however. Not wanting them to get wet, she picked up the dollhouse and the box of paper dolls, and carried them around the house to the front porch.

By the time Flossie returned to the back yard, Freddie had the hose attached. He told his sister to hold the nozzle while he turned on the water.

"Look out!" he cried, as the water suddenly spurted out.

Now, Flossie had held the hose in her hands many times before, but never had the water been turned on full force all at once. In an instant, the long, coiled hose slipped through her fingers. It twisted and jerked like a great snake until it straightened itself out.

In the meantime, the water shot in every direction. First it squirted at Waggo's kennel, soaking it. Waggo was the Bobbseys' lively fox terrier. He slept outdoors in his little house, and kept watch over the property. At present, luckily, Waggo was off playing with some other dogs.

Next, the water soaked some dresses of Flossie's which were hanging on the line.

"Oh, oh!" cried Flossie. "Turn it off, Freddie! Quick!"

Freddie was trying to, but turning on the water seemed easier than turning it off. While he was struggling with the faucet on the side of the house, the stream of water shot into a flower bed and uprooted several pansy plants.

Flossie had been jumping from place to place, trying to pick up the end of the wriggling hose. Finally she jumped squarely upon it with both feet. The next thing the twins knew—*psst!*—a spray of water shot straight into the air from just behind where the little girl was standing. The hose had burst!

Freddie was frightened now, and yelled for Sam. The colored man came running out the kitchen door, and in the twinkling of an eye turned off the water.

"My, my!" he exclaimed. "Freddie Bobbsey, what mischief yo' gwine git into next?"

Freddie explained that he had merely wanted to squirt the hose on the sails of his new windmill to make them go round. Sam grinned and admitted that this was not a bad idea. He went into the garage, got a pair of garden shears, and cut off the ruined piece of hose. Then he attached the nozzle to the good part and told Freddie to hold it near the windmill.

Sam turned on the water again but only a little at a time. The force of the water finally became great enough to make the wings of the windmill go around gently. Sam laughed merrily.

"I guess I brought yo' a waterwheel 'stead of a windmill," he said. "Now don't play with it very long, or dere'll be a puddle here."

The twins promised to be good, and Sam hopped into the truck and backed out of the driveway. As he drove down the street, Flossie said she thought they should turn off the water right away.

"Aw, we just started to play," Freddie objected. Then he laughed. "I was going to wash the glue off my hair and my sweater with the hose," he said.

"Oh," cried Flossie, "you can't do that!"

"Why can't I?" her brother asked. "I'll do my hair first."

He leaned over and directed the stream of water onto his head. He gasped as the cold water ran down his neck and over his clothes. It hit Flossie as well, and soaked her.

"Freddie, you're an awful boy!" she screamed. "Now we'll have to change all our clothes."

"Indeed you will," said a voice from the kitchen door.

Stout Dinah came puffing toward the children. Freddie looked up. The next instant, the poor colored woman was drenched too. Quickly she turned off the water, then scolded the twins for making such a mess.

"Dere's as much water in dis here yard as dere is in Holland," she told them. "An' I declare, de place looks like Holland right now, wid dat windmill sittin' right in de middle of it."

Flossie and Freddie had heard about Holland in school. They knew it was 'way across the ocean, and that there were lots of water, pretty flowers, and windmills. Also, that some of the people wore shoes made of wood. This was enough to stir Freddie's imagination.

"Let's play Holland," he suggested to Flossie.

"Yo'll do nuthin' o' de sort," said Dinah firmly. "It's a warm day for May, but not warm enough to mess in water. Yo' chilluns go right upstairs an' put on dry clothes."

Before going inside, Flossie decided to run around and gather up her paper dolls. She would not be playing with them again today. As the little girl reached the front porch, she stared in blank amazement.

The paper dolls were nowhere in sight. Even the box was missing!

CHAPTER II

THE MYSTERIOUS VISITOR

"DINAH! Freddie! Come here quick!"

Flossie Bobbsey was so excited at the loss of her paper dolls that she began to jump up and down. But it was not Freddie or Dinah who answered her call. Up the street came a boy and a girl about twelve years of age. They were Bert and Nan, Flossie and Freddie's older brother and sister.

Nan and Bert were twins also, but did not look like Freddie and Flossie. They had brown hair and eyes, while Flossie and Freddie had blonde hair and blue eyes.

"What's the matter?" Nan called, running up.

Flossie explained that, a few minutes before, she had set not only her dollhouse but Susie and her entire paper family on the porch.

"The wind couldn't have blown my dolls away, because there wasn't even enough wind to turn the wings of Freddie's new windmill," Flossie finished.

10

"Windmill?" cried Bert. "Where is it?"

"In the back yard," Flossie answered. "But, please, Bert, help me find my paper dolls."

Bert glanced quickly around the porch and the front lawn. Not seeing the paper dolls, he went off to the back yard.

Nan made a more thorough search with Flossie. Though they looked all along the street and in the neighbors' gardens, there was not a trace of the paper dolls. The girls asked several people on the street if they had seen them, but no one had had even a peek at the missing dolls.

"But you'll find them," said Mrs. Smith, a neighbor who lived a few houses down the street. "You Bobbsey children seem to be able to solve all your little mysteries."

What Mrs. Smith said was true. The two sets of Bobbsey twins, who lived in a big, old-fashioned house in Lakeport, were always having adventures of one sort or another. They had gone on exciting trips with their parents to many places, even as far away as Mexico. And during the time they were at home, going to school or playing with their friends, interesting and amusing things often happened to them.

Only recently they had helped an elderly toy mender who had broken his wrist and was unable to go on with his business. In the end, the toy mender's workshop became known as the Bobbsey Twins' Toy Shop. What fun and excitement developed before they solved the mystery of Bert's ship model!

Now Flossie wondered if she ever would solve the mystery of the paper dolls. She decided that someone must have taken them.

"It could even be Waggo," she told Nan.

Waggo was a mischievous little fox terrier, but the children loved him and always forgave him for his pranks, because they had so many good times with him.

Nan and Flossie hurried to Waggo's kennel in the back yard. There was no sign of the paper dolls, nor of Waggo either.

"Do you s'pose Waggo took them away?" Flossie asked her sister.

Nan smiled. "Let's play detective," she said, "and look for Waggo. Maybe we can find out where he went."

The girls walked through three back yards and into a field. A little brook ran along the far end of the field. There they found Waggo having a fine time playing in the brook with a dog playmate.

When the fox terrier saw Nan and Flossie, he bounded out of the water and made straight for them. He shook himself so vigorously that he showered them with water, all the while wagging his tail very hard.

"Did you take my paper dolls?" Flossie asked him. "Maybe for a swim?"

Waggo cocked his head. Nan said she was sure he was surprised at the question and was not guilty.

Flossie agreed. With a sigh, she added, *"Now where shall we go detecting?"*

Her sister said they had not yet looked in the house. It was just possible that Dinah had picked up the paper dolls. But when the girls reached home, Dinah said she had not touched Flossie's dolls. The search continued, but not one of them was found.

"Oh dear," said Flossie, as they finally gave up the hunt, "I wonder if we'll ever find them."

Nan went outside to see Freddie's new windmill. She and Bert were studying about Holland in school, and just that day they had seen pictures of the big windmills which dotted the country.

Their teacher Miss Vandermeer had told how the windmills did all sorts of work: how they pumped water, sawed wood, ground wheat into flour.

Nan was surprised at the size of the toy windmill. It was two feet high and looked just like the pictures of real windmills. Bert was working on it to see if he could make the wings spin easier.

"I'm going to take this to school for our Holland project," he told Nan. "Isn't it swell!"

Freddie was not sure he wanted Bert to borrow his toy, but Bert promised to take very good care of it.

"Everybody's going to bring something to Miss Vandermeer's class," Bert said. "But I'll bet nobody else will bring a windmill."

"What are you going to take, Nan?" Flossie asked.

Her sister pointed to a flower bed near the front of the yard, where there were several beautiful tulips in bloom. The flowers were pink, white, and yellow. Nan had planted the bulbs the fall before, and she was very proud of her garden.

"In Holland," Nan told Flossie, "the people grow millions of tulips to sell, and they send the bulbs to this country."

Dinah, who had come out of the house, walked over and gazed at the flowers.

"Dey's beautiful," she commented. "Yo' will have de best flowers in de whole classroom."

Dinah thought everything the Bobbsey family did was just about the best anybody could do.

"I don't know whether they'll be the best tulips," Nan said, "but, anyway, I'm glad they bloomed. It's the prettiest garden I've ever had."

Dinah and the small twins went into the house. Bert continued to tinker with the windmill, and Nan went to sprinkle water on her tulips so that they would be perfect for picking early the next morning.

Suddenly a voice near them said, "Say, you kids probably are in Miss Vandermeer's class, aren't you?"

The twins looked up and Bert said, "Yes."

"Where does she live?" the stranger asked.

Bert did not like the man's looks, and he thought it was funny that the stranger should come to the Bobbsey house for information. He was just going to ask the man why he wanted to know where Miss Vandermeer lived, when Nan said:

"On Hester Street."

"What number?"

"I don't know," Nan replied. "It's a brown house with a fence around it."

"How about you kids showing me where it is," the stranger suggested.

Bert did not like the man's manner. "Before we show you her house, tell us why you want to know where Miss Vandermeer lives," he said.

The man gave Bert a rather crooked smile. "You're a smart kid," he remarked. "Miss Vandermeer is an old friend of mine. I just heard that she lives in Lakeport."

"How'd you know we're in her class?" Bert asked him.

"I didn't, but I figured you probably went to her school," the man answered. "Well, come on now. Show me where she lives. I'm in a hurry."

Although neither of the twins liked the stranger, they could see no good reason why they should not grant his request. They walked down the street, turned the corner, went two more blocks, and pointed out the house where Miss Vandermeer boarded.

"There it is," said Bert, and added suddenly, "What's your name, sir?"

"Sam Tomson," the man replied. "Now are you satisfied?"

Bert did not answer him. He and Nan turned and walked up the street. Bert's curiosity got the better of him in a few seconds, however, and he turned around. He fully expected to see Sam Tomson on the porch of Miss Vandermeer's home, ringing the doorbell. To his amazement, the man was nowhere in sight.

"Gee, that's funny," Bert remarked.

"It certainly is," said Nan. "I don't believe that man is a friend of Miss Vandermeer's at all. Let's go back and tell her about him."

CHAPTER III

THE WOODEN SHOE RACE

"OH, HELLO, Bert. Hello, Nan," Miss Vandermeer said, as she opened the front door. "I'm glad to see you. Won't you come in?"

The twins followed her into the living room.

"Do you have a friend named Mr. Sam Tomson?" Bert burst out.

The teacher looked surprised at the question, and said she knew no one by that name. She asked Bert why he wanted to know, and he explained about the stranger who had come to the Bobbsey home.

"That's very strange," Miss Vandermeer said. "Are you sure that was the name?"

"Yes," Nan spoke up. "We thought he was coming to see you right away."

"No one has been here," their teacher said, still looking puzzled.

"We didn't like the man," said Bert, "so I'm glad he's not a friend of yours."

As the children turned to go, Nan smiled at the teacher. "I just love what we're having in geography now," she said. "I think Holland must be a lovely place."

Miss Vandermeer looked pleased. "I'm glad to hear you say that," she answered. "To me, Holland is one of the loveliest places in the world. But probably I think that because my family came from Holland."

"Oh, they did?" the twins asked in chorus.

The teacher said that she still had many relatives in Holland; in fact, her family had lived there for hundreds and hundreds of years.

"Maybe Mr. Tomson came from Holland," Nan suggested.

"I don't think so," said Miss Vandermeer. "Tomson is not a Dutch name. Oh, well, we won't worry about him."

But Bert did worry about Sam Tomson. He could not get the man out of his mind as he and Nan left Miss Vandermeer and walked back along the street toward their own home. Perhaps the man was all right, but the boy could not forget his sneering smile and strange behavior.

Next morning Bert was the first one up. After breakfast, he dusted off the toy windmill to take to school. His father adjusted a screw, and the arms spun around freely.

"Oh, thanks, Dad," Bert said. "Now it's perfect."

"Sam fixed up most of it after you went to bed," Mr. Bobbsey told him.

In the meantime, Nan had walked into the yard to pick her tulips. Their Holland project was going to be fun, especially since she had her beautiful pink and white and yellow flowers to enter as her contribution. Suddenly she stopped short and stared in amazement.

"My tulips! They're gone!" Nan cried.

Not a tulip was to be seen. Nothing was left of the pretty flowers but tiny bits of stems which stuck up from the ground.

"Mother! Mother!" she cried, running into the house. "Somebody has taken my tulips!"

Mrs. Bobbsey questioned everyone in the house. No one knew anything about the missing flowers. She put her arm around her daughter.

"It's a shame," she said.

Mrs. Bobbsey felt very sorry for Nan, because the little girl had taken such good care of her flowers. And now, when the big moment to display them had arrived, they were gone!

Dinah was as much upset as Nan. "Well, I never!" she declared. "Dey was de prettiest flowers in de whole world. If I ever find out who took 'em, I'll—I'll—"

Dinah stormed out to the kitchen without finishing her threat.

"Now I have nothing to take to school for our Holland project," Nan said, tears in her eyes.

"Wait," said Mrs. Bobbsey. "I think I have just the thing for you, Nan. Something Daddy brought from Holland years ago."

Eagerly the Bobbsey twins followed their mother upstairs to the attic. She pulled an old chest from under the eaves and opened it. Rummaging to the bottom, she pulled out a pair of strange-looking shoes.

"They're wooden!" Flossie exclaimed.

"They must be *klompen,*" Nan said.

"What's a klomp-klomp?" Freddie asked, taking one of the wooden shoes in his hands.

The others laughed.

"Klompen," Bert said, "is the name for wooden shoes which some of the Dutch people wear—especially the children."

"Holland has so much water in it," Nan explained, "that the ground is often damp. The wooden shoes keep the children's feet from getting wet."

Mrs. Bobbsey closed the attic door and they all hurried downstairs.

"You can take the klompen to school for your project," Mrs. Bobbsey said to Nan.

Nan thanked her mother, all the time wondering who could have taken her tulips. On the way to school, Nan talked it over with Bert.

"I have an idea," her twin said. "I'll bet it was Danny Rugg."

Danny Rugg, who lived near the Bobbseys, was a boy about the same age as Bert and Nan. He was in their class at school. Danny took delight in teasing the small children, and in playing mean tricks on the older ones.

When the school bell rang, Flossie and Freddie hurried to their classroom. Bert and Nan eagerly burst into theirs, Bert carrying the big windmill and Nan the klompen. Their classmates crowded around Bert.

"Does the windmill really work?"

"Where did you get it?"

"Make the wings go round."

Bert spun the wings.

"Gee, it's swell," said his friend Charlie Mason, who had brought a bar of Dutch chocolate as his exhibit.

Just then Nan grabbed Bert's arm. "Look, Bert!" she exclaimed.

Her twin glanced across the room. There stood Danny Rugg, proudly holding a bouquet of pink, white, and yellow tulips. Bert set the windmill on his desk and approached Danny.

"Where'd you get those tulips?" he asked.

"You don't have to know," Danny replied.

"Somebody picked Nan's tulips from her garden," Bert said.

"So what?" Danny replied rudely. "She hasn't the only tulips in the world."

Before Bert could question him further, Miss Vandermeer entered the room and the boys and girls hurried to their seats. The teacher was very glad to see all the souvenirs of Holland that the children had brought. One boy had a pair of "balloon" trousers. A friend of Nan's had brought a miniature of the Royal Palace in Amsterdam.

At Miss Vandermeer's request, the children put their trophies on a long table in the front of the room. Then she told them about Holland, and how the brave Dutch people had pushed back the sea to gain miles and miles of land on which to live and grow things.

"It was done by building high walls, called dikes," she said. "Then windmills pumped the water over the dikes and into the sea."

"Did they have windmills hundreds of years ago?" Bert asked.

"Yes, indeed," his teacher replied. "The windmills have been a big help to the Dutch people.

Today electric pumps are used in many places instead of windmills."

"Why do they still keep the windmills, if they have electric pumps?" Nan asked Miss Vandermeer.

"Well, for one thing, they're very pretty to look at," her teacher replied. "But mainly, it's to help the people remember how much courage their ancestors had when they pushed back tons of water so they'd have land on which to live."

Then Miss Vandermeer told about klompen. She explained how the wooden shoes were made and how the children wore little velvet boots inside the shoes. Miss Vandermeer was delighted that Nan had brought a pair of klompen.

"Where did you get them?" she asked.

"Daddy brought them from Holland many years ago," Nan said.

"I think they are big enough to fit you children," Miss Vandermeer said. "Come here, Bert, and try them on."

The klompen fitted Bert perfectly. Just then, John Marsh, another friend of Bert's, raised his hand.

"I brought a pair of klompen, too," he said.

"Suppose you get them," Miss Vandermeer suggested, "and try them on."

John went to the long table where he had set his wooden shoes. He took off his own shoes and put on the klompen. Then, to the delight of the children, John and Bert walked around the room going *klomp, klomp, klomp*. They sounded like a team of horses on a cement road.

"Wouldn't it be fun to see the boys run?" said Nellie Parks, a friend of Nan's.

"Oh, yes! Let's have a race," Nan suggested eagerly.

The boys grinned.

"That would be quite a sight," Miss Vandermeer agreed. "We'll have a race during recess."

Miss Vandermeer ended her discussion of Holland by telling the children about her own home near Lake Michigan.

"My relatives came from the Netherlands," she said, "and settled in Michigan with many of their countrymen, in a beautiful place they called Little Holland. I lived with my uncle and aunt, who own a large tulip farm."

Miss Vandermeer smiled. "You'd love the farm. Part of it is on a little island, and is just like a real Dutch farm, with a windmill, and a cheese house, and beds built in the wall."

"Oh, it sounds wonderful," Nan Bobbsey spoke up.

"It is," Miss Vandermeer answered. "If any of

you should ever go to Michigan, I'm sure Uncle Pieter and Aunt Hilda would be glad to see you."

At recess the children ran into the grassy schoolyard. Miss Vandermeer marked out the length of the racecourse for Bert and John. Then she explained the rules.

"If your klompen come off," she said, "you will be disqualified."

As she was explaining this, Danny Rugg, unnoticed by the two boys, slipped up close to Bert, then sneaked back into the crowd of children.

The two boys took off their shoes and put on the klompen.

"Ready! Set! Go!" Miss Vandermeer said, as the other children cheered.

Bert and John ran fast, lifting their feet high. The klompen felt like heavy boots. Suddenly Bert began to stumble.

"Oh! I can't run any more!" he cried, and fell to the ground.

CHAPTER IV

BERT IN TROUBLE

NAN AND several boys hurried to Bert's side.

"What's the matter?" Nan cried anxiously.

Bert had removed one of the klompen. As he held it up, a large pebble dropped from the toe of the wooden shoe.

"How did that get in there?" Bert cried.

He was angry and puzzled. There had been nothing in the shoe when he put it on earlier. Had someone deliberately tried to keep him from winning?

As he got up, Bert looked directly at Danny Rugg. He was the only boy in the class who would have played such a trick. Bert wanted to have it out with Danny then and there, but decided to wait until after school.

A bell in the building rang, and Miss Vandermeer called to the children to return to their classroom. At the same moment a little boy came dashing up to Bert, who was still holding the klompen.

"What are you doing here?" Bert asked in surprise.

The little boy was his brother Freddie, who had left his own classroom.

"I saw it from the window!" Freddie cried excitedly.

"Saw what?" Bert asked him.

Freddie pointed directly at Danny Rugg. "He put something in one of your klompen that made you fall down."

"I did not!" Danny exclaimed.

"You did too," Freddie insisted. "I saw you out the window. When Bert put his shoes down, you put something inside one of them!"

Freddie's loyalty to his brother made him forget all the rules of the school. He not only had left his classroom without permission, but now he went up to Danny and punched him on the chin.

"Why, you little squirt!" Danny exclaimed.

With that, he gave Freddie a push that knocked him off his feet. Instantly Bert and Charlie Mason rushed at Danny, and a real fight started.

"Stop it!" cried Miss Vandermeer. "Stop it!"

There was so much confusion that the fighters could not hear her. Finally Nan, knowing there was trouble ahead, dashed to Bert's side and told them to stop.

Miss Vandermeer lectured the boys severely. She sent Freddie back to his classroom, where he was roundly scolded by his own teacher for leaving his class without permission.

Bert, Charlie, and Danny were made to stay after school. Miss Vandermeer finally got Danny's admission that he had put the small stone in Bert's klompen.

"But I was only having some fun," Danny sniveled.

"Playing harmless jokes on others is one thing," Miss Vandermeer told him sternly, "but to deny having done it is a serious offense. I hope that after this you will tell the truth, Danny."

Bert hoped that Danny would now tell him whether or not he had taken Nan's tulips. But Danny still stoutly declared that lots of people had the same kinds of flowers in their gardens.

In the meantime, Nan had started for home with the klompen that had caused all the excitement. When she was about halfway there, she saw a strange sight. Running toward her were two little dogs. One was Waggo. Both dogs were dripping wet, and in Waggo's mouth was a little live fish.

"Waggo, Waggo!" Nan shouted. "You mustn't swallow that fish. The bones might stick in your throat."

She coaxed Waggo to come to her, but the little dog was having too much fun with the fish to give it up. He flipped it into the air. His little dog playmate grabbed the fish and scampered around in circles. Waggo dashed after him and got it back.

"Please! Please, Waggo," Nan begged.

But the mischievous fox terrier could not resist the temptation to run off with his new plaything.

"He must have caught the fish in the brook," Nan decided.

She ran after the dog, but the terrier skipped this way and that, heading for the Bobbsey home. When Nan finally caught up with him, Waggo was sitting in front of his kennel, gleefully thumping his stubby little tail. Before his furry paws lay the fish, with a little life still left in it.

"Look how the poor thing is gasping," Nan scolded.

Just then Freddie and Flossie ran up.

"Waggo caught a fish," Nan told them.

"Without a hook?" Freddie's eyes popped wide.

"We'll have to watch and see how he does it, next time," Flossie said.

"Let's take the poor thing back to the brook," Nan suggested.

"Oh, let me get a pan of water to put him in," Freddie said.

The little boy rushed to the kitchen, returning with a saucepan of water. He put the fish in the pan. Then the Bobbseys hurried to the brook.

"One! Two! Three! I'm going to throw him in!" Freddie shouted, when they reached the bank.

"No, don't do that," Nan warned. "It might hurt him. Just put him in gently."

Freddie lowered the little fish into the brook and took his hand away. The fish rolled over on its side, worked its gills in and out, flipped its tail, and darted away.

"There he goes!" Flossie exclaimed happily.

The children returned home. Bert was just coming from school. He called excitedly to Nan:

"I saw Mr. Tomson!"

"Where?"

"Downtown."

Bert felt he should tell Miss Vandermeer at once about the man, and find out whether the stranger had ever come back to see her.

"Let's go to her home right now," the boy suggested.

The twins hurried to the teacher's home. The woman who owned the house opened the front door and said Miss Vandermeer was upstairs.

When the teacher came down, the twins no‑ ticed that she was holding a fairly large book in her hand. She showed it to them, explaining that it was very, very old and worth a great deal of money.

"It's full of pictures," Nan remarked.

"Yes," Miss Vandermeer said. "They are orig‑ inal drawings by a very famous Dutch artist. He was a friend of my great‑grandfather and made this book especially for him."

Bert and Nan were intrigued by the drawings. Some of them were pictures of Dutch fishermen. Others were of children skating. Nan especially liked one picture, an elderly man watching two children doing a klompen dance.

"The boy and girl look just alike," she re‑ marked.

Miss Vandermeer said they were twins and that the girl was her own mother. "The old gen‑ tleman is her grandfather, the man for whom the artist made the book of pictures. It was presented to him on his sixtieth birthday."

"They're the loveliest pictures I've ever seen," Nan said, as she finished looking through them.

Miss Vandermeer smiled. "I wouldn't part with this book for all the money in the world," she said, "even though any one picture in it could be sold for several hundred dollars."

"Wow!" Bert cried. "I should think you'd be afraid to leave the book around."

"Perhaps I am foolish," Miss Vandermeer agreed, "but I love to look at the pictures, and the other people in this house do, too."

She laid the book on the table, and then said she had received an interesting letter that afternoon from her aunt.

"You recall, Aunt Hilda lives out near Lake Michigan. She wants me to come to the *Tulpen Feest,* which is going to be held soon. But, of course, I won't be able to go."

"What is the Tulpen Feest?" Bert asked her.

The teacher said it was the "Festival of Tulips." She explained that in the area near Lake Michigan, where her relatives lived, there were many farmers whose ancestors had come from Holland. They had brought with them the secret of growing beautiful tulips.

"The tulips are in bloom now," Miss Vandermeer said. "Millions of them."

"Oh, I'd love to see them!" Nan cried. "It must be wonderful to see a million flowers in bloom all at once."

"It surely is," the teacher answered. She sighed. "I haven't been to a Tulpen Feest in years. It is a four-day holiday for everyone. There are parades and games and dancing, all done in the costumes of olden days in Holland."

"Oh, I hope I can go there sometime," said Nan. Then she giggled. "The people ought to make the tulips bloom in the summertime, so children and their teachers can go see them after school is out."

Miss Vandermeer smiled and said that, unfortunately, the tulips bloom only in cool weather. With another sigh, she added, "Maybe sometime I can take a special vacation in May, and join my friends at the Tulpen Feest.

"This year there's to be a special celebration. Usually there are no prizes, but a lovely old lady is donating some very fine possessions of hers. She says she wants other people to enjoy them, and this is the way she has chosen to give them away."

"What are the prizes?" Nan asked.

"I don't know, except the grand prize," Miss Vandermeer answered. "That is a small pair of gold klompen studded with diamonds. My aunt has seen them and writes me that they are very beautiful."

Suddenly Bert dashed to the window. Then he raced toward the front door.

"What is it?" Miss Vandermeer asked.

"That man!" Bert cried. "Mr. Tomson. I—I saw him sneaking off the porch!"

CHAPTER V

HELPING THE POLICEMAN

THE TEACHER looked startled at Bert's words. She followed him to the front porch, with Nan right behind her.

"Why'd the man go away?" Nan asked excitedly.

"It is strange," Miss Vandermeer said.

Bert looked up and down the street but could not see Mr. Sam Tomson. The house was only one door from the corner. No doubt he had gone down the side street.

The twins ran to the corner, but Sam Tomson was nowhere to be seen. Puzzled, but sure the man definitely was no friend of their teacher, they went back to her house.

"I can't understand this," Miss Vandermeer exclaimed. "You say, Bert, this Mr. Tomson was sneaking off the porch?"

"Yes, Miss Vandermeer, and I'll bet he was looking in the porch window, too."

Since the window was open, Bert added, it was probable that the mysterious man had heard the conversation between the teacher and the twins. Miss Vandermeer said she did not think Mr. Tomson was necessarily a suspicious person. Perhaps he merely had come to call. Upon learning she already had visitors, he might have decided to wait until another time to see her.

Bert and Nan left the house. Bert was convinced that Sam Tomson was not a person to be trusted, and told his sister so.

"Why should he go sneaking off the porch if he's okay?" the boy insisted.

Bert's hunch proved to be right. Early the next morning the Bobbsey telephone rang. Miss Vandermeer was calling Bert. She was very much upset.

"My valuable book of pictures was stolen last night!" she said.

"What!" Bert exclaimed.

Miss Vandermeer explained that she had forgotten to take the book back upstairs to her room. During the night someone had cut the screen and opened the window from the porch into the living room. Several articles had been taken, among them the book she prized so much.

"I believe now that you were right about that

Mr. Tomson," she said. "A detective is here. Would you and Nan come over and give him a description of Mr. Tomson?"

"Yes, indeed," Bert replied. "We'll come right away."

He returned to the breakfast table and told the rest of the Bobbsey family what had happened.

"Oh!" cried Nan. "That beautiful book! Why, Daddy, Miss Vandermeer said every picture in it was worth hundreds of dollars."

"And there were lots of pictures," Bert added.

Freddie and Flossie were wide-eyed. They insisted upon going along with Nan and Bert to hear what the detective would ask them. There was still plenty of time before school.

Mr. Bobbsey, who was ready to leave for his office, said he would drive the children to their teacher's house. When they reached it, he went inside with them.

The twins recognized the detective who was in the living room talking to Miss Vandermeer. He was called Jim by all the school children. They knew him because as a policeman he had stood near the school crossing to direct traffic. He had been promoted and now was a police detective.

"Hello, twins," he greeted the Bobbseys as they walked in. "Good morning, Mr. Bobbsey." Then he looked at Bert and said, "I understand a man came to your house the day before yesterday, asking where Miss Vandermeer lived. What did he look like?"

Bert told him. Then Jim asked Nan. She agreed with Bert's description that Mr. Sam Tomson was about a foot taller than Bert, rather thin, and had dark hair. But Nan thought he had blue eyes while Bert thought they were brown.

"I can tell you one thing," Bert spoke up. "He smiled out of the corner of his mouth."

Freddie wondered how one could do this, and immediately began to practice. Flossie laughed at the funny faces her twin was making. He kept saying, "Like this?" But each time, Bert would say, "No."

Finally Bert showed the others what he meant. The policeman thought that this was a very good clue to identify Sam Tomson.

"It's what we call a crooked smile," he said. "And now tell me what kind of clothes he was wearing."

The twins could recall nothing unusual about his clothes. He had worn a dark suit, dark tie, and a straw hat.

Jim turned to Mr. Bobbsey, "Would you be willing to lend me your twins today?" he asked

"All of us?" Freddie spoke up eagerly, jumping up from the chair on which he sat.

What fun to be borrowed by a policeman! The little boy had no idea of where they might go or what they might do. But this did not matter. Just to be with Jim would be more exciting than anything he could think of.

"Sorry, little man," the detective said. "I meant just Nan and Bert. I'd like to have them go around with me a bit and see if we can find this Sam Tomson. Will it be all right with you, Mr. Bobbsey, and you, Miss Vandermeer, if Bert and Nan stay away from school this morning?"

The twins' father and their teacher were sure the school principal would not count Bert and Nan absent if they were helping the police department do something for Miss Vandermeer.

Jim already had questioned the teacher and the other people who lived in the house about the theft. He also had examined the front porch, the window, and the window sill. So he was ready to leave.

"We'll go on our hunt in my car," he told Bert and Nan.

Freddie was very envious of his brother and sister. He watched them as they drove out of sight. He told Flossie that as soon as school was out, he was going to play policeman.

"And when I grow up, I'm going to be a policeman," he said.

"I thought you were going to be a fireman," Flossie teased her twin. "Or a candymaker, or a cowboy."

With each new adventure, Freddie always met some grownup whose work he admired. Each time, he decided to be just like that person. Right now he could think of nothing more exciting than to be a police detective.

"If you want to be a policeman after school," Flossie suggested, "you can hunt for my paper dolls."

"A lady policeman ought to do that," Freddie remarked. "But I'll do it."

The little twins climbed into Mr. Bobbsey's car and were driven to school. In the meantime, Nan and Bert were cruising around Lakeport in the police car.

"Keep your eyes open," Jim told them. "Suppose you look on the left side of the street, Bert," he suggested. "Nan, you take the right."

They went up one street and down another. Many men were hurrying along to their offices and stores. But Mr. Sam Tomson was not among them.

"Maybe he took a train," Bert spoke up finally.

"You might be right, son," Jim agreed. "But

sometimes thieves stay around just to pretend they are innocent."

"You mean," Nan asked, "that if a person who took something stays around, other people will think he's innocent because he didn't run away?"

Jim said that was exactly what he meant, and for this reason there was a good chance the suspicious stranger was still in town. He said the police already had asked at the hotel and at boardinghouses if a Mr. Sam Tomson were staying there. But no one by that name had been at any of those places.

"Sometimes people don't use their right names," the police detective told the twins. "So the next thing we'll do is go around to those places and ask if a man with a crooked smile was staying there under some other name."

When they reached the Lakeport Hotel, Jim asked Bert to show the clerk how Sam Tomson smiled. The clerk said no one answering the description had stayed there, but he thought Bert was a very good mimic.

"You ought to go on the stage when you're a little older," he told the boy with a laugh.

Nan laughed, too. The Bobbseys had thought of doing many things but never of going on the stage as mimics. As the twins left the hotel with

Jim, Nan asked Bert to think up an idea for a twin act.

"How about you and me smiling crooked smiles out the sides of our mouths?" he said. "Then we could stand side by side. I'd talk out of one side of my mouth and you'd answer me out of the other side of yours."

Jim said he would like to see this. So before they got into the car, Nan and Bert tried it. The act looked so silly that Jim roared with laughter. But finally he said:

"Come on now. Back to work."

The twins climbed into the car and they proceeded down the street to a boardinghouse. They had gone only a few feet when Bert cried out:

"Look! There's Sam Tomson!"

"Where?" Jim asked quickly.

Both Nan and Bert pointed to a house down the street. A man had just come down the steps and was hurrying up the block. The detective put on a burst of speed, but was delayed in traffic at the corner. By the time they started up again, the suspect had gone into a store. Jim pulled up to the curb and stopped the car. He and the twins rushed into the store.

At the counter stood a man about a foot taller than Bert. He had on dark clothes and a straw hat. In his hand he held up a bright red necktie.

"Is this the man?" Jim asked the Bobbsey twins.

Bert gulped. "N—no, sir," he stammered.

The boy felt very foolish over his mistake, and Nan did, too. They realized that they would have to do better than just spot someone who was a foot taller than Bert and who wore a dark suit and a straw hat.

They returned to the car with the police detective and once more started for the boardinghouse. Suddenly a voice came over the police radio in Jim's car.

"Calling car twenty-one."

"That's us!" Jim told the twins.

"Calling car twenty-one. Suspect seen in railroad station. Proceed there at once. That is all."

While Nan and Bert held their breaths, Jim turned on his siren and raced to the railroad station.

CHAPTER VI

THE DARK CAVE

PEOPLE stood still. Cars pulled to the curb, as the Bobbsey twins raced in the police car toward the railroad station.

Upon reaching it, police detective Jim got out quickly and raced into the building. Nan and Bert were close behind him.

"All aboard!" they heard a train man shout.

"Hold it!" Jim called.

He and the twins hustled aboard and sat down at the end of one of the coaches.

"Is—is Mr. Sam Tomson on board?" Bert panted. "Is that why we came?"

"Your guess is as good as mine," the police detective answered. "We'll start through the train looking for him. Bert, suppose you and I go through the rear cars and look. Then, if we don't find him, Nan and I will walk through the forward cars. We'd better hurry."

Jim and Bert went from one coach to another

in the swaying train. Mr. Sam Tomson was not among the passengers.

A few minutes later the police detective and Nan started their hunt in the forward part of the train. But they had no better luck. The man who was suspected of having stolen Miss Vandermeer's rare book of pictures was not on the train.

At the next station, Jim and the twins got off. After a few minutes' wait, they boarded a train going in the opposite direction and soon were back in Lakeport.

The police detective drove the Bobbseys home, and thanked them for their morning's work. He told them to keep their eyes open whenever they were downtown, in case Sam Tomson should still be around.

"What should we do if we see him?" Nan asked.

Jim thought a moment. "Well," he said, "try to get a policeman. But if you can't, see if you can find out where Sam Tomson goes, and let me know."

Nan and Bert had lunch, and then went to school. They told Miss Vandermeer of the morning's chase.

"But we didn't find the man," Nan told her.

"We're going to, though!" Bert declared stoutly.

After school the twins wondered what had become of their small brother and sister. They usually met Freddie and Flossie each afternoon coming out of the building.

But today Freddie had persuaded Flossie to start for home the minute they got out. He reminded her that they were going to play policeman.

"And find my paper dolls," she said gleefully.

Freddie's friend Harry Ford had promised to lend him a policeman's suit which he had worn on Halloween the year before. When they reached Harry's house, Freddie insisted upon putting on the suit.

"Oh, you look just be-yootiful!" Flossie exclaimed.

"Huh," Freddie said in disgust. "Policemen don't look beautiful. They look—they look—"

Freddie could not think of the right word. But he felt that a policeman would stand very straight, with his head held high, and be very smart. Above all, he should carry a whistle—a very *loud* whistle. Freddie felt in the pockets to see if there was a whistle. There was. He blew a loud blast on it.

"Come on, lady. We'll find your children," he told Flossie, and marched down the steps from Harry Ford's house.

Flossie giggled. Now she was a grown-up lady with a lot of paper children! She followed Freddie down the street.

All went well until they came to the corner. Freddie was so busy holding his head up high that he missed the curbstone completely. Down he went, right on his face!

"Oh dear!" Flossie ran to help her twin. She brushed off his policeman's suit and wiped the dirt from his face with her handkerchief. "You look all right now," she told him, "only your badge is bent."

Freddie's nose hurt because he had hit it pretty hard, and he was not sure that he could carry on his work so well with a bent badge; but he decided to try, anyway.

"Let's go through the fields all the way to the brook, and look for your children," Policeman Freddie suggested to Lady Bobbsey.

"Okay," Flossie agreed.

Freddie turned his steps toward the brook which babbled along some distance to the rear of the Bobbsey property before it ran into the park lake.

About halfway there, Freddie suddenly stopped. He bent down and picked up a piece of paper.

"Here's one of your children!" he exclaimed.

"You'd better take her to the hospital," he added solemnly.

In his hand Freddie held one of the missing paper dolls. She was a sorry sight, indeed—certainly ready for the paper doll hospital. One arm was torn off, and half her hair was gone. Besides this, she was covered with mud.

"Oh, you poor thing!" Flossie exclaimed, taking the doll. "How did you ever get here?"

Freddie was already walking ahead, looking for the doll's brothers and sisters. In a few moments he came upon one of the boy dolls. He looked even worse than the one Flossie held in her hand. His face was a smeary red, white, and blue, and he had no legs!

Flossie simply stared. Then tears came into her eyes. She decided then and there that she did not want to find the rest of her paper children. It was all too sad.

But Freddie did not feel that way about it. He had begun to think he was a very clever policeman.

"I'll find your children for you, lady," he said. "If they've lost too many legs, and their faces have run off, I'll make new ones for you."

"Where are you going now?" Flossie wanted to know, without accepting Freddie's offer to fix her paper children.

Freddie stood still and considered. Then he grinned.

"To the secret place," he replied.

"The secret place? What's that?" Flossie demanded.

Freddie did not tell his twin, for the simple reason that he did not know, but he was sure that was what a police detective would say. When Flossie insisted, however, he said:

"The cave."

Flossie became interested in the hunt all over again. She knew there was a small cave down by the brook. It was a favorite place for boys to play. Maybe the rest of her paper dolls were there and unharmed!

"I'll go with you," she announced.

The twins marched through the field, keeping their eyes open for more paper dolls. But they found none. It took them nearly an hour to locate the cave. Some older boys, who had been playing Indian there, had blocked up the entrance.

"Oh, Freddie," said Flossie, "how are we ever going to get into the cave?"

"That's easy," Freddie said importantly. "You just help me pull these boxes away."

The little twins pulled and tugged at the top box. Finally they knocked it over. By the time they had pulled two others away, Flossie was very tired.

"Let's go home," she pleaded.

"No," said Freddie. "I'm going inside the cave and find your children!"

The little boy started to crawl in. It was very dark, but in a few moments he could see the interior better. There were some empty cans and a couple of crates. In a far corner of the cave stood a shoe box.

"I'll bet I've found them!" Freddie's muffled voice came to Flossie's ears.

Flossie got down on her knees and looked inside the cave.

"What did you find?" she asked excitedly.

Freddie was already crawling toward the shoe box. At that moment a gruff voice outside the cave cried:

"Get out of there!"

CHAPTER VII

THE EARTHQUAKE

FREDDIE Bobbsey did not hear the gruff voice ordering the small twins away from the cave. He kept on crawling toward the shoe box, because he now felt sure that if Flossie's missing paper dolls were anywhere in the cave, they were in that box.

His sister jumped up and turned around to see who had spoken. It was Danny Rugg!

"What are you doing here, Flossie?" the boy demanded in a disagreeable tone.

Suddenly it occurred to Flossie that maybe Danny did not know Freddie was inside the cave. If she could get Danny to go away, he would not find her brother. Then, if the paper dolls were inside the cave, Freddie could get them and bring them home.

"I'm not doing anything," Flossie replied to Danny. "I was just taking a walk."

"Girls aren't allowed in this cave," Danny said. "It's a pirates' den."

Flossie wanted to know what a pirate was. She looked a little frightened as Danny told her a horrible story about men who wore black patches over one eye and carried whips and made other people give up their jewelry and money and even their toys.

"Maybe Mr. Tomson is a pirate," said Flossie.

"Who's he?" Danny asked.

"The man who took Miss Vandermeer's book."

Danny got the whole story from Flossie. While she was telling it, the little girl kept walking away from the cave. By the time she finished, they were a good distance from it.

Flossie had looked back several times, wondering whether or not Freddie had come out of the cave. She was sure that if he had found the paper dolls and then seen Danny, he would have run home a different way.

"Why'd you come down here, Danny?" Flossie asked, carrying on the conversation so that she could give Freddie plenty of time.

"None of your business," the boy replied abruptly, "and you go on home."

When Flossie reached the Bobbsey house, Freddie was not there. Flossie was worried. She went at once to find Bert and ask him to go back with her to the cave. She said she was afraid her twin might be in trouble with the pirates.

Upon hearing the story, Bert wondered if Flossie had not stumbled upon the solution to a mystery which had puzzled the boys at school. Baseball gloves, bicycle horns, and various other bits of personal property had been disappearing. Maybe they had been taken by a group of boy pirates who had their headquarters in the cave!

"Why don't you stay home and let me handle this myself?" Bert suggested.

But Flossie would not do this. If Freddie was in trouble, she was going to help him!

As she and Bert hurried down the street, they met Charlie Mason. Bert immediately told him the story and asked him to go along.

"You bet," Charlie said. "It'd be swell to find all those things that have disappeared. And it would be a good joke on Danny!" he added gleefully.

When they came to the cave, Danny was not in sight, and no one else seemed to be around.

"Maybe the pirates are inside," Flossie said.

Bert told her to stay out while he and Charlie went in. Flossie stood very close to the entrance, however, so that she might run for help if necessary.

There was no one in the cave. Bert and Charlie tried to investigate the place, but could see little.

"Gee, I wish we had a flashlight," Charlie remarked.

"I'll get one from Susie," Flossie offered.

Her friend Susie Larker lived in a house not far from the cave. Flossie ran all the way to Susie's, and borrowed a light. Susie was very much excited when she heard why Flossie wanted the flashlight, and insisted upon returning with her.

Bert beamed the light around. Suddenly he exclaimed:

"This is the pirates' cave, all right!"

"It sure is!" Charlie cried excitedly. "Here's John Marsh's bat. See his initials?"

Charlie and Bert found several other articles which had been taken from the boys at school. Most of the pirates' loot had been laid back on rocks in the sides of the cave. Anyone who just happened to wander in would not be apt to see it.

"Shall we take these things away?" Charlie asked Bert.

"Sure," Bert replied. "Let's take them to my house, and call up the fellows they belong to."

As the two boys gathered up baseball equipment, sirens, penknives, and several good-luck raccoon tails which their friends carried on their bicycles, Bert grinned.

"Danny and his pirate friends sure are in for a surprise," he said.

"You bet," Charlie agreed. "Shall we come back sometime when they're here, and fight 'em?"

Bert thought a moment. He and Charlie would not make out very well against a whole gang of pirates.

"I'd rather play a trick on the pirates," Bert finally answered.

"That's a good idea." Charlie laughed. "How about printing a sign and hanging it on the cave, so they'll find it there when they come back?"

"Swell," Bert said, "but we'll have to hurry. The pirates may be here any time."

Flossie, who was trotting along beside the boys, had almost forgotten about Freddie. Suddenly the little boy appeared from behind some trees, holding a shoe box in his hand. He still wore the policeman's costume.

"Has Danny gone?" he asked, rather frightened. "Say, where'd you get all that stuff?" he added excitedly.

When Bert told him it had been in the cave, Freddie looked surprised. He had run out of the cave as soon as he found the shoe box.

Flossie opened the box and looked inside it. There lay her missing paper dolls!

"Danny did take them," Bert said, upon seeing the dolls. "I'll bet he came to our house to look at Nan's tulips and saw your paper dolls on the porch, Flossie. He thought this was a chance to be a pirate, and took them."

"And dropped two of them in the field," Flossie spoke up. "Oh, Freddie, you're a wonderful policeman detective. You said you'd find my paper dolls and you did."

"You did more than that," Bert praised his small brother. "You put the pirates out of business!" Bert snapped his fingers. "That's what we'll put on the sign, Charlie," he said.

When they reached home, Bert got a piece of cardboard and printed on it:

PIRATES' DEN CLOSED!
FORCED OUT OF BUSINESS ON
ACCOUNT OF NO LOOT!

Charlie got some strong twine and tied it through two holes punched near the top of the cardboard. Then the two boys hurried back to the cave. Still no one was there. Quickly they hung the sign on a rock which stuck out from the front of the cave.

Just as they finished, Bert and Charlie heard voices in the distance. They scooted off and hid behind some of the bushes that lined the edge of the brook. In a few moments Danny Rugg and three other boys appeared.

As they neared the cave, one of them pulled a black patch from his pocket and adjusted it over one eye. Danny began to crack the whip he was carrying.

At this very instant the four boys spied the sign. They stopped short and stared. Bert and Charlie could hardly keep from laughing.

The other boys were too stunned even to speak. Finally Danny demanded:

"Who put that sign there?"

"Don't know a thing about it," one of his friends replied, and the other two said they did not know either.

With a cry of rage, Danny bent down and went inside the cave. The others followed. They did not stay long, and when they came outside the four of them were arguing loudly. Danny took down the sign and tore it up. He threw the pieces into the brook, and they floated right past Bert and Charlie, who were choking back their laughter.

"It's your fault, Danny Rugg," one of the other boys cried out. "You thought it would be fun to play pirate. Now you've got us all in trouble."

Danny told the others that they were just a bunch of sissies. This started a fight, which Bert and Charlie did not wait to see. Keeping out of sight behind the bushes that lined the brook, they made their way to the Bobbsey house. There they telephoned to the boys who owned the loot, and asked them to come over at once.

When the other boys heard the story, they roared with laughter. They all decided to keep Danny and his friends guessing about who had found the loot. Freddie came in for a great deal of praise for having thought of the cave, and he and Flossie promised not to let Danny learn that they knew anything about the pirates.

At dinner Mr. and Mrs. Bobbsey heard the story, and chuckled about it. Nan, too, laughed, but she said:

"I still think Danny took my tulips, and I don't care if he did it to play pirate or not. It was a mean trick."

"Speaking of tulips," said Mr. Bobbsey, "I'm making a trip to the Michigan lumber country in a few days. I may have time to stop in the section where the tulips grow, and bring you some bulbs."

Nan told her father about the Tulpen Feest which would soon take place. She also mentioned that Miss Vandermeer's old home, which was so interesting and beautiful, was in the same area.

"Oh, I want to go to the Tulip Land!" Flossie cried out.

The others smiled. This was a very good name, indeed, for the famous territory.

"I wish you all might go with me," her father said, "but I couldn't take you out of school."

Freddie made a little sound in his throat which was a cross between a grunt and a sigh. "Oh, phooey with school!" he exclaimed.

"Why, Freddie!" his mother said severely.

Bert explained that in Tulip Land the children have a four-day holiday during the Tulpen Feest.

"So we ought to have a holiday, too," Freddie insisted.

The others laughed. Freddie went right on, becoming so enthusiastic on the subject of going to Michigan that he almost made himself believe he was on his way there.

That night Freddie dreamed that a big helicopter landed on the roof of the school and took all the children to Tulip Land. When the little boy woke up, he was very much disappointed to find himself still in Lakeport. But after he got to school, he forgot about his dream.

At eleven o'clock that morning, while Bert and Nan were listening to Miss Vandermeer tell more about life in Holland, Nan suddenly realized that her desk was shaking. Quickly she looked over toward Bert. He had a strange expression on his face.

Miss Vandermeer stopped talking. The next second, a little vase of flowers on her desk crashed to the floor. At the same time some of the Dutch exhibits rolled off the long table.

A moment later the whole school building shook. Miss Vandermeer grabbed a corner of the desk to keep her balance. A look of alarm crossed her face, although she tried not to show it.

"What's happening?" Nellie Parks cried out.

"I'm afraid," Miss Vandermeer replied shakily, "it's an earthquake! Quick, children! Get under your desks!"

CHAPTER VIII

A SURPRISE

IN another part of the school building, Freddie and Flossie and their classmates were huddled under their desks. The children were very much frightened, and many of them were crying.

Just as the Bobbsey twins were beginning to cry, too, the building stopped shaking. The pupils were told to remain where they were, however, for several minutes longer. Then the room telephone bell tinkled. Their teacher answered, then turned to the children.

"You are to leave quietly, just as you do in a fire drill," she said. "Get your coats and go to the schoolyard at once. Remain there until you are told what further to do."

When the small twins reached the school field, they stood on tiptoe, looking for Bert and Nan. The older twins were doing the same thing, and were very much relieved to see their little brother and sister safe. They all waved to each other.

The school principal came from the building.

Standing on the top step, he told the pupils how thankful he was that the earthquake had been a slight one and that no one had been hurt. They were to go home immediately and report to their parents, who undoubtedly were worried about them.

"It is not known," the principal added, "how much the shaking may have weakened this building. You will not return to classes until you have been notified."

Freddie felt gleeful. Maybe, if the school were closed, they could go to Tulip Land with Daddy!

When he said this to his brother and sisters, as they hurried along the street, Bert and Nan did not answer. They were worrying about their parents, and Dinah and Sam. Maybe something had happened to them in the earthquake!

The children saw many broken windows, and in two stores canned goods had fallen from shelves in the windows and crashed through to the sidewalk. To the twins' relief, they found very little damage at home. A few dishes had been broken, and an apple pie Dinah had just baked had toppled from a table and squashed on the floor.

Mrs. Bobbsey and Dinah were all right and had already telephoned the school to make sure the children were safe. Mr. Bobbsey also had

telephoned that he and the others at the lumberyard were not hurt. He was relieved to learn that
the twins were all right too, and requested that
they stay at home for the rest of the day.

Late that afternoon, the Bobbsey telephone
rang. Charlie Mason was calling Bert.

"Did you hear the good news?" Charlie asked
excitedly.

"About what?"

"No school for at least two weeks!"

"What!" Bert cried.

Charlie's father was on the Board of Educa-
tion. An inspection of the school building had revealed that the earthquake had damaged it con-
siderably. The school had been built many years
before, and the violent shaking had weakened
part of the structure.

"Gosh," said Bert, "that's swell. I mean it's too
bad about the building, but it's swell to have a
vacation."

Nan, who was standing near by with Freddie
and Flossie, demanded to know what Bert had
just heard. When Bert told them, Freddie let
out a yell like a fire siren.

"Now we can go to Tulip Land!" he shouted.

Seeing his father coming in the front door, the
little boy made a flying leap and landed in Mr.
Bobbsey's arms.

"My goodness," Mr. Bobbsey said. "Take it easy, little fireman. You act as if you were on your way to a fire!"

Daddy Bobbsey had been calling his small son his little fireman for some time. Ever since babyhood Freddie had loved fire engines.

"Well, what is it?" Mr. Bobbsey demanded.

"My dream came true," Freddie announced.

"Your dream?" his father asked, puzzled.

Freddie told how he had dreamed of going to Tulip Land in a helicopter. Now, since he did not have to go to school for some time, there was no reason why he and his brother and sisters should not go to Michigan with their father.

"Whoa, whoa!" Mr. Bobbsey said, laughing. "Let me hang up my coat and then we'll talk about it."

"I'll hang up your coat," Freddie offered. He wanted to show his father how helpful he could be.

The entire Bobbsey family gathered in the living room to discuss Freddie's idea. The twins' father finally said that, while he would like to take his wife and children with him to Michigan, he was not sure if he could get train reservations at such short notice.

"But, Daddy," Flossie said, climbing onto his lap, "you can try, can't you?"

"Why, yes," her father replied. "Do you want to go as much as your twin does, my fat fairy?"

Flossie giggled. She was only a little girl, but she already had learned that when Daddy called her by this favorite nickname, he was on the verge of granting a wish of hers. Now she hugged him very tightly.

"Course I want to go as much as Freddie," she said. "Oh, we'll have such fun."

Mr. Bobbsey turned to his wife. "Well, Mother," he said, "what do you think? You know I shan't be able to be with you all the time in Tulip Land. Do you think one person can manage two sets of twins who get into all sorts of funny situations?"

Mrs. Bobbsey gave her husband a knowing look. Then she smiled.

"The children and I have been away from home several times without you," she said. "If you can get hotel reservations, it won't take me long to pack."

"Oh, that's wonderful!" Nan cried, giving her mother a kiss.

Bert was thrilled to go on the trip, but he wondered what else there might be for him to do in Tulip Land except look at flowers and watch a parade. Suddenly a thought came to him. It was just possible that they might be able to visit

Miss Vandermeer's old farm home. At that moment Nan said:

"Dad, don't you think it would be nice to ask Miss Vandermeer to go with us?"

"I think it would be very nice," her father agreed. "She could show you around and no doubt point out things which you might otherwise miss."

Mrs. Bobbsey liked the idea. She went to the telephone and spoke to the teacher, who laughed merrily.

"You must have read my thoughts," she said. "I have just telephoned the airport to see about getting a reservation."

Mrs. Bobbsey said that they had not considered going by plane.

"If you don't fly out," Miss Vandermeer told her, "you may not get there in time for the Tulpen Feest. There are no train reservations for a week; I have just found that out."

Mrs. Bobbsey asked about the hotels in Tulip Land. Miss Vandermeer gave her several names, but said that people usually made reservations far ahead, and she hoped that they had not all been taken.

"I'll be glad to see what I can find out," the teacher told Mrs. Bobbsey. "I'm going to telephone Aunt Hilda after dinner and tell her I'm coming. She and Uncle Pieter will know whether the hotels will have room for more visitors."

Upon hearing this, Flossie and Freddie begged to be allowed to stay up until she called back. They and the older twins talked constantly after dinner, while they were waiting for the teacher to telephone. Bert kept hoping that if Miss Vandermeer found a place it would be near the island farm.

Freddie went to the garage where his toy windmill had been put. It was very heavy for him to carry, but he thought it ought to be in the house in honor of a possible trip to Tulip Land.

Although the little boy had turned on the garage light, he had forgotten to snap on the one for the porch. When he returned to the house, it was very dark on the back steps. He had nearly reached the top step when he slipped. The toy windmill flew from his arms and rolled down to the ground.

Freddie lost his balance and crashed down on top of it. There was a loud, splintering sound and a cry from the little boy.

A moment later the porch light was snapped on and Dinah rushed out.

"Mah land, chile!" she exclaimed. She hurried down the steps. "Well, I'se glad yo' didn't break yo' head!"

She helped the little boy to his feet. By this time the other Bobbseys had come outside. Mr. Bobbsey examined his small son. The boy was all right, but the windmill was smashed. Freddie could never play with it again.

"It's a shame about your nice toy," his mother said kindly. "But maybe—"

Freddie looked up at her, tears in his eyes. "Maybe what?" he asked.

She told him that surely out in Tulip Land there must be very fine toy windmills for sale.

"If we shouldn't be able to go there ourselves," Mrs. Bobbsey said, "at least Miss Vandermeer might buy you a windmill and send it home."

As she finished speaking, the telephone rang.

"Maybe it's Miss Vandermeer," Bert exclaimed, dashing into the house.

It was the teacher calling. She told Bert she had very good news for him, and also a big surprise.

"What is it?" Bert cried eagerly.

"Well, suppose you ask your mother to come to the telephone," Miss Vandermeer said. "I'd like to tell her about it first."

CHAPTER IX

FLYING TO TULIP LAND

THERE was complete silence in the Bobbsey living room while the twins' mother talked with Miss Vandermeer. All the children could hear was:

"Yes—oh, my goodness! Are you quite sure it's all right?—Well, it's certainly very kind of you —Four lively children—"

Finally Freddie could not stand the strain any longer. He jumped from his chair and ran to his father.

"What *is* Mother saying?" he asked. "It—it sounds awful mysterious."

Daddy Bobbsey laughed. "You're an impatient little fireman," he said. "You'll have to wait."

To Freddie's relief his mother said good-bye at that very moment. The twins rushed to her side.

"Tell us!" they pleaded. "Please hurry and tell us what she said."

Mrs. Bobbsey flopped down in a chair. She looked at her husband, then at the children, shaking her head from one side to the other.

"Wonders will never cease," she said at last.

"Is it bad?" Flossie asked, wide-eyed.

"No, indeed. It's very wonderful," her mother replied. "Miss Vandermeer has made arrangements for us to go with her to Michigan."

"By plane?" Mr. Bobbsey asked.

"Yes."

"Was she able to get hotel accommodations for you and the twins?" her husband wanted to know.

"That's the wonderful part of it," Mrs. Bobbsey replied. "We're invited to stay at her uncle Pieter's farm."

"We're what?" Bert cried. He could hardly believe such good fortune. "You mean, we've been invited to visit the island farm?"

"Yes. But I wonder if we should accept," she replied.

"Oh, Mother!" the twins cried together. "Why not?"

Mrs. Bobbsey did not answer immediately. Instead, she asked Mr. Bobbsey what he thought about accepting the invitation.

The twins' father chuckled. "Miss Vandermeer must think a lot of Bert and Nan, or she wouldn't want to take them to her family's farm,"

he said. "But Freddie and Flossie—" Mr. Bobbsey paused.

"Oh, I'll be good. I promise!" Freddie cried.

"I will, too," Flossie spoke up quickly. "I
won't be a—a sissy or a crybaby or anything that
Freddie says I am sometimes."

"Then in that case," their father said, "I'd say
it would be all right for you to accept."

"Wow! That's swell!" Bert yelled.

"It's super," Nan said.

As for Freddie, he turned a somersault, while
Flossie jumped up and down, clapping her hands
and singing:

> *"We're going to Tulip Land!*
> *We're going to Tulip Land!*
> *I want to go as fast as I can!"*

Nan began to sing, too, then she asked when
they would be leaving.

"Day after tomorrow," her mother answered.
"And now, Freddie and Flossie, to bed you go!"

For once the small twins did not object. They
raced upstairs. Freddie went to the room in
which he slept with Bert, and Flossie tripped off
to the pretty little corner room she shared with
Nan. But before being tucked in by their mother,
both children looked through their closets and
bureau drawers for clothes to wear at the farm.

Freddie pulled out some old overalls. "I might

milk a cow," he told himself, "and if I do, I'll need these."

Flossie thought a flowered dress might be good for Tulip Land, but then she decided that it did not matter about dresses. What was more important was to keep her feet from getting wet.

"I haven't any klompen," she thought, "so I'll take my snow boots."

When Mrs. Bobbsey heard her small daughter's idea, she laughed. "I'm afraid your feet would get pretty hot in these fur-lined boots in May," she said. "Just rubbers will do, and you won't even need them unless it rains."

In no time at all it was day after tomorrow; suitcases were packed, and the Bobbsey family was ready to leave.

"I'se gwine miss yo' sumpin' terrible," Dinah declared, as she served them an early breakfast. "An' Waggo, he's gwine be lonesome too."

Waggo did look sad. The little fox terrier had sniffed at the suitcases, and seemed to know that the children were about to leave him. He did not wag his stubby tail as he usually did. He just sat still in the dining room looking from one child to another.

Finally Flossie called Waggo over and hugged him tightly. "We won't be gone long," she told him. "The Tul-tul—"

"Tulpen Feest," Nan helped her out.

"It's only four days," Flossie said, "and I'll tell you what. Mother, may Waggo have a special bone every day we're gone?"

Mrs. Bobbsey said Dinah could arrange this with the butcher. Flossie felt better, and was sure Waggo did, because he began to wag his tail again.

"I beg yo' pardon, Mr. Bobbsey," a voice said from the doorway. It was Sam. "It's gettin' late. I believe yo' all better hurry."

Mr. Bobbsey glanced at his watch and said that Sam was absolutely right. They must leave in five minutes.

What a scramble! The children ran to put on their coats. Sam carried the small suitcases to the car and put them into the trunk compartment—he already had taken the large bags to the airport earlier.

In the excitement Waggo went along, too. He had jumped into the trunk compartment when no one was looking. At the airport he hopped out and ran toward the plane. But Sam scooped the fox terrier up in his arms, and said that he would not let him get away again.

Miss Vandermeer was waiting for the Bobbseys. She went aboard the big airplane with them, and they took their seats. Freddie was glad he was right across the aisle from the teacher. She could tell him all about her uncle Pieter's cows. After the plane zoomed into the air, he leaned over and said:

"Do your uncle's cows give chocolate milk?"

Several people who heard Freddie smiled. But Miss Vandermeer seemed to understand what he meant.

"You're thinking of Dutch chocolate, which is made with milk, aren't you?" she asked.

"Uh-huh," Freddie replied.

"Dutch chocolate is made by mixing chocolate and milk and sugar in a special way," the teacher said. "But milk is always white." Then Miss Vandermeer asked, smiling, "Did you ever hear the old joke, Freddie, about the brown cow that ate green grass and gave white milk?"

By the time the trip to Tulip Land was half over, Freddie and Flossie thought Miss Vandermeer was just about the nicest teacher anyone could have. They hoped she would still be at their school by the time they reached her grade.

Miss Vandermeer told them a little more about her uncle's farm. "It's very large. The house and barns are on the island, with a canal going completely around the property. Then, in the fields beyond, are the tulips my uncle grows."

Although the Bobbsey twins had a pretty good

idea of the Vandermeer farm, it proved to be quite different and even more interesting than they had thought.

Mr. Bobbsey hired a taxi to take them from the airport to Uncle Pieter's place. For a mile before reaching the farmhouse, the road wound in and out through vast fields of tulips in bloom. First they came to a field with nothing but yellow tulips as far as the eye could see. Then they drove through another with nothing but red flowers.

"I've never seen anything so gorgeous," Mrs. Bobbsey gasped.

"I'm certainly glad I came along with you," Mr. Bobbsey said. "Even though I can't stay, I would hate to have missed this wonderful sight."

The twins' father was leaving on a train the next morning to go into the lumber country. He would return in a few days to take them home.

"There's my uncle's island," Miss Vandermeer said, a few minutes later.

The whole Bobbsey family gasped. They had never seen anything so quaint and attractive! Over the little canal was a rustic wooden bridge. Not far from it stood a large windmill. Its four wings were turning lazily in the soft breeze.

"Oh!" Freddie cried. "The windmill's as big as a house!"

"Yes," said Miss Vandermeer. "Often people live in them. But my uncle uses his for storing tulip bulbs."

The taxi clattered over the bridge and sped toward the house. It was a two-story building, almost completely covered with ivy. Peeping out through the ivy were many windows and doorways framed with rustic wood.

Tulips and other flowers bloomed in profusion everywhere one looked. Neat, white gravel paths wandered among the flowers.

Off at a distance stood two barns. They had large barnyards completely surrounded by snow-white fences. Everything was as neat as a pin.

As the taxi drove up to the house, the door opened and a rosy-cheeked, elderly woman came out. She wore a large white lace apron. Around her shoulders was a matching scarf and on her head was a bonnet of the same material. It was turned up at the outer corners and neat gray curls peeked from beneath it. She smiled at the visitors.

"Aunt Hilda!" Miss Vandermeer exclaimed, jumping from the taxi.

She introduced the Bobbseys to her aunt, one by one. The small twins half expected Aunt Hilda to speak Dutch, but she greeted them in perfect English.

"I am so glad to have you visit us for the Tulpen Feest," she said. "I hope you have a very pleasant stay while you're here."

She led them into the living room of the quaint house. It looked exactly like pictures of homes in Holland that Bert and Nan had seen recently in school.

Near a large stone fireplace stood a spinning wheel. On the mantelshelf was a row of blue-and-white plates decorated with scenes of people skating on the Holland canals. When Freddie spied the plates, he asked Mrs. Vandermeer if her island canal ever froze over so that they could skate on it.

"Yes, indeed," Aunt Hilda replied. "It gets very cold here in the winter."

Miss Vandermeer and her aunt showed the Bobbseys around the house. Mr. Bobbsey brought in the baggage and set it down where Mrs. Vandermeer directed.

Flossie had looked and looked for beds upstairs. Seeing none, she wondered where the visitors were supposed to sleep. Finally she asked Miss Vandermeer.

"Remember, I told you that my uncle likes to live exactly the way his father did in Holland. In that land, many of the beds are in the wall. That's the way they are here. I'll show you."

She pushed aside a wall panel in one of the

rooms. Two beds, one above the other, were built right into the wall!

"By having the beds in here," Miss Vandermeer explained, "they don't take up space in the room. And in the wintertime there are no drafts."

Flossie looked up at the teacher and smiled. "I like that," she said. "At our house, when we have the windows open in the wintertime, it gets cold too. I have to put my head under the covers to keep warm."

When the group gathered in the living room again, Aunt Hilda remarked that Uncle Pieter and the children would be home soon.

"What children?" Freddie asked.

Mrs. Vandermeer smiled. She turned to the teacher and said:

"I forgot to tell you on the telephone that Dirk and Wanda are here."

"Really?" Miss Vandermeer asked in surprise. "How wonderful!"

She told the Bobbseys that Dirk, a boy of twelve, and Wanda, his ten-year-old sister, were her nephew and niece. Their home was in Holland.

"And they're visiting here?" Nan spoke up excitedly.

"Yes," Aunt Hilda said. "I'm sure you'll love both of them."

CHAPTER X

MISCHIEVOUS CALVES

A CLATTER outside the Vandermeer house drew the twins to the window. A large cart drawn by two horses was stopping at the door.

On the high seat sat an elderly man with a jolly smile. He looked even more like a picture-book person than Mrs. Vandermeer did, with his balloon trousers and a high, round, cloth cap perched on the back of his head. In his mouth was a long, white clay pipe.

Next to him was seated a pretty little girl who wore a costume very much like Mrs. Vandermeer's. On the other side of the girl sat a boy dressed like the man. All three wore wooden shoes.

Miss Vandermeer opened the door and hurried outside. "Uncle Pieter!" she exclaimed. Then she gathered the little girl into her arms. "Wanda! How wonderful to see you." She put up one hand and squeezed the boy's arm. "Dirk, how fine you look!"

They all trooped into the house and were introduced to the Bobbsey family. Nan thought she had never seen a prettier girl than Wanda. And Dirk certainly was a handsome lad. They both had bright-red cheeks and clear, blue eyes, revealing their very good health.

To the twins' delight, both children from Holland spoke excellent English, with only a slight accent, and politely asked if the Bobbseys had had a good trip.

"Did you come here in an airplane?" Freddie asked them.

"No," Dirk replied. "We came across the ocean to New York on a big ship, and then we took a train to Michigan."

"We call this place Tulip Land," Flossie said.

"That's a very good name," Mrs. Vandermeer said. "We've never given the farm a name. I believe Tulip Land would be a good one for it."

"Do you always wear these clothes?" Flossie asked Mr. Vandermeer.

The farmer chuckled, took the pipe from his mouth, and told her that he wore them only once in a while.

"But when I knew you were coming, I thought I'd put them on today."

"I'm glad you did," Mrs. Bobbsey spoke up. "It is like being in Holland itself."

Dirk and Wanda said that they never had owned any American clothes, but were going to buy some before they went home. Wanda took Nan and Flossie to her room where the girls were going to sleep. She showed them several pretty dresses she had brought with her from Holland. With each cotton dress she wore a different colored apron, and she had several caps, some gaily colored, some white.

Wanda was rather tall for her age, and though she was only ten, was as big as Nan. Suddenly Nan had an idea.

"Instead of buying an American dress," she said, "how would you like to exchange some clothes with me?"

Wanda thought that this was a lovely idea, and immediately each girl put on a dress belonging to the other.

"It's not zackly fair," Flossie remarked. "Nan is getting an apron and a scarf and a hat extra."

"You're right," Nan agreed, and took a scarf from her suitcase to give to Wanda.

When the two girls were ready, they marched into the living room, where the older people were talking.

"Well!" Mrs. Vandermeer said, laughing. "It didn't take you long to change places."

"Nan, you ought to go in the Children's Parade," Mr. Vandermeer said. "You certainly look the part of a little Dutch girl."

"Oh, do you think I might?" Nan asked eagerly.

The Vandermeers were sure it would be all right, and immediately the Bobbsey twins began planning what they might wear. It would be easy for Bert to borrow one of Dirk's outfits, but what could they do about Flossie and Freddie?

Kindly Mrs. Vandermeer said she would work out something, even if she had to make the clothes herself. Although the Children's Parade was only a few days off, she was sure she and Mrs. Bobbsey could get something ready in time.

Dirk and Wanda took the Bobbsey twins for a tour of the island farm. As they went from place to place, they found everything extremely neat and clean. Wanda explained that people in Holland, and also their relatives in the United States, like to keep everything spotless. The barns particularly interested Bert and Freddie. In one, hay was piled carefully in the loft, and several horses stood in shiny stalls.

In the other barn stood six cows whose hides glistened. In a corner box stall lay two baby calves.

"I wish I had a calf," Freddie sighed. "Maybe I can play with one of these."

He opened the door of the stall. Instantly the two calves got up and loped out.

"Oh, Freddie!" Nan cried. "You shouldn't have done that."

The two calves already were making their way toward the outer door, which was open. The four older children tried to capture them. But the calves leaped into the air, their hind feet nearly kicking the boys in the face.

Unfortunately, Freddie, who had been the last one to enter the barnyard, had not closed the gate. Now the calves raced outside, frisking about.

"Oh!" Nan exclaimed suddenly to Dirk and Wanda. "The calves will ruin all your aunt Hilda's beautiful flowers!"

Flossie shut her eyes. She could not look at the sight. The two calves seemed to be playing some kind of game as they jumped around crushing the beautiful tulips.

"Get out of there!" Bert yelled.

In their excitement, Dirk and Wanda called to the animals in Dutch. *"Ga weg!"*

But the happy calves paid no attention to the shouts in either language.

The children's cries brought the grownups from the house. To the twins' surprise, Farmer Vandermeer calmly picked up one calf in his arms, while his wife picked up the other. They carried them to the barnyard and locked them in.

Freddie was trying not to cry. Only a few minutes before everything had been so beautiful in the flower garden. Now it was a sorry sight. And it was all his fault, Freddie thought, horrified.

Before the little boy's mother had a chance to say anything, Freddie went up to Uncle Pieter and Aunt Hilda. "I'm terrible, terrible sorry," he said. "M-maybe you'd better p-punish me."

The farmer and his wife were so surprised at such a request that they began to laugh. Uncle Pieter told him that any little boy who owned up so quickly was a pretty fine sort of fellow.

"Instead of punishing you," Uncle Pieter said, "I'm going to let you help me clean up this damage and plant some new tulips."

"I want to help, too," Flossie called out.

"All right," Uncle Pieter told her. "In fact, I believe all of you might be interested in learning something about tulip growing."

"We never sell any flowers," the farmer continued, after he sent Dirk for a basket. "We just raise the bulbs to sell."

When Dirk returned, Uncle Pieter directed Freddie to pick up all the ruined flowers, stems, and leaves which had been trampled by the calves. He himself took the bulbs out of the soil and put them into the big pockets of his jacket.

Then he asked Wanda and Dirk to go to a little shed back of the main house and bring him back several potted tulips. He planted them where the other flowers had been growing, and within fifteen minutes no one would have known that the mischievous calves had been in the garden.

As Nan looked on, she thought of her own tiny tulip garden at home. Beside these big, beautiful flowers, hers would look like baby tulips.

"If Danny Rugg did take my tulips, when he was playing pirate, he didn't get much!" she decided, with a smile.

The Bobbsey twins would have liked to inspect the windmill, but it was suppertime, and they were told that they would have to wait until the next morning. The children enjoyed the delicious food, which included large slices of homemade bread with jelly, and cookies in all sorts of fancy shapes. At the end of the meal, Aunt Hilda passed around bars of Dutch chocolate which she had made.

"I just love to make candy," Nan said. "Will you please show me sometime how to make Dutch chocolate, Aunt Hilda?"

"I'll be glad to," Aunt Hilda replied. "Suppose we do it tomorrow."

The twins thought going to bed at Tulip Land

Farm was a lot of fun. They slid back the wall panels hiding their sleeping quarters, and climbed up. Nan and Flossie slept on one side of the girls' bedroom, while Wanda climbed into a wall bed on the other. Bert and Freddie slept one above the other in the boys' room, while Dirk was on the opposite side.

"It's like being on a train," Freddie remarked. He had once slept on a train. "Only this bed stands still."

"That's right," Dirk called across. "It's not like the berth I had on the ship crossing the ocean."

Bert wanted to know if the ship had rolled much. Dirk said indeed it had. Once, when the ocean became rough, he had rolled right out of bed.

"But I didn't hurt myself," he added.

All the children slept soundly, and awoke to a beautiful, sunny morning. They dressed quickly and went outside. Each one went off by himself for a little while to look at what interested him most. Bert headed for the windmill. Freddie ran to look through the barnyard fence. Nan stayed in the house to watch breakfast being prepared. When it was ready, she ran outside to call the others.

They did not come at first, because her voice

did not carry far enough for them to hear it. But finally Bert showed up, then Freddie, and at last Dirk and Wanda.

"Where's Flossie?" Nan asked.

All said that they had not seen her. They shouted together loudly. Still Flossie did not appear.

By this time Mr. and Mrs. Bobbsey had come from the house. Upon learning that their small daughter was missing, they looked at each other anxiously. They hoped the little girl was not in any danger.

CHAPTER XI

BOILING CANDY

EVERYONE on Tulip Land Farm began to hunt for Flossie Bobbsey. Bert and Freddie went to the big barn and climbed up into the haymow. Their little sister was not in the hay.

Nan and Wanda went to the windmill and looked inside. The little girl was not there.

In the meantime, Mr. and Mrs. Bobbsey and Miss Vandermeer had started to walk along the bank of the canal.

Dirk and his great-aunt and -uncle began hunting in the tulip fields beyond. They called and called, but no answer came.

Finally Uncle Pieter and Aunt Hilda returned to the island to see if there was any report on the missing child, but Dirk went on and on through the fields. He passed the group of red flowers, and presently came to the field where the yellow tulips were growing. Suddenly he stopped short and stared ahead. Something yellow was moving among the tall flowers. Yes, it was the golden hair of a little girl.

"Flossie! Flossie!" Dirk cried out.

"Oh, hello," Flossie answered in a matter-of-fact voice. "Where's everybody?"

Dirk, who had run forward, looked at the little girl in amazement. Then he said:

"Don't you know you're lost?"

"Me lost?" Flossie said. It was her turn to be surprised.

Dirk told her that she had frightened everyone and that her family, as well as the Vandermeers, were out looking for her.

"I'm sorry," Flossie said.

"Breakfast is ready," Dirk said. "Aren't you hungry?"

Just about to answer him, Flossie suddenly screamed and jumped to one side. At the same instant, Dirk leaped forward. Quick as lightning, he leaned down, grabbed a snake from the ground, and snapped it in the air. Then he threw it down. The snake lay motionless.

"Now it won't hurt you," he said to Flossie. "Come on. I'm hungry."

Flossie followed quickly behind Dirk. The farther they walked, the more the small twin realized how far off she had wandered. She gave a little shiver. If Dirk had not come at that very moment, the snake might easily have bitten her!

"I'm not going away by myself any more," she said suddenly.

As they came across the bridge, Flossie's parents ran to meet her. Seeing that the little girl was all right, they asked where she had been. When Dirk said he had found her over half a mile away from the island, they all wondered how she could have got there so quickly.

"I guess it must be the good air in Tulip Land," Flossie replied. "I felt just as if I had wings like a fairy." She turned to Mr. Vandermeer. "I just wanted to see all your beautiful flowers," she explained. "I like the yellow tulips the best. What's their name?"

The tulip farmer said that particular variety in the field where Flossie had met the snake had not been named yet. Then he chuckled and asked:

"You wouldn't want me to call it the Snake Tulip, would you?"

"Oh, no! Please don't do that," Flossie replied. "I don't think anybody would buy Snake Tulips."

"I guess you're right," Mr. Vandermeer said. "And now, let's go to the house. Your daddy has to leave soon."

While they were eating breakfast, the Bobbsey twins asked Dirk and Wanda what games they played in Holland and how the children spent their days.

"I guess we play some of the same games you do," Wanda replied. "But in the wintertime we do more skating. We skate to school and to church and to all the parties we go to."

Dirk said that sometimes a teacher would take her whole class on an ice holiday. There were regular skating courses held for different age groups.

"Boys my age," Dirk told them, "can skate all day without getting tired."

"And girls, too," Wanda spoke up.

Nan and Bert thought this amazing. They could skate for perhaps three hours at a time, but they were sure they never could stand an all-day trip on the ice.

"Do you skate?" Wanda asked Freddie and Flossie.

The small twins had to admit that they could just about stand up on one-runner ice skates. Until very recently they had used the two-runner variety.

"In my country there is so much ice in the wintertime," Wanda told them, "that everyone has to skate to get around. So almost as soon as babies can walk, their parents put them on skates."

Freddie asked what else they did in winter.

Wanda told him that at Christmastime they had a wonderful celebration.

"But, you know," Miss Vandermeer spoke up, "in Holland most of Christmas Day is spent in church. It is on St. Nicholas Day, December sixth, that the children have their joyous celebration. On the Eve of St. Nicholas, Santa Claus rides through the night leaving gifts at each house."

Flossie giggled. "I guess it takes Santa Claus all the rest of the time to get from Holland to our country," she remarked.

The others laughed. Miss Vandermeer said that in Holland Santa Claus is called *Sinterklaas,* and that he does not come by himself, as he does in the United States.

"He brings a dark-skinned young man along to help him leave gifts for the children," the teacher explained.

"I've seen pictures of the American Santa Claus," Wanda said. "He comes in a sleigh that's pulled by eight reindeer, doesn't he?"

"Sometimes he comes in an airplane," Freddie said. "I guess that's when he's in a special hurry."

"Our Sinterklaas comes on a white horse," Wanda told the twins. "On the Eve of St. Nicholas, we always leave hay and carrots for the horse to eat."

Miss Vandermeer told of another difference in the Christmas custom. In America children hang up their stockings, but in Holland small gifts are put into their klompen, which they leave in front of the fireplace.

"When I lived in Holland," Aunt Hilda said, "no one put Christmas cards on gifts. It was just as if Sinterklaas had left lovely presents for grownups, too. What actually happened was that friends left gifts on one another's doorsteps, without saying whom they came from."

"Didn't you ever find out who gave you the presents?" Nan asked.

Aunt Hilda said that people usually found out, but not for a long time. But it was fun to guess, and the longer one could fool his friends the more fun it was.

Mrs. Vandermeer rose from the table and the others followed her to the garden. One of the men who worked for Uncle Pieter brought a car to the door. Mr. Bobbsey got in and waved goodbye.

"I'll see you all sometime next week," he said.

Wanda and Nan went back into the house. The Dutch girl said that when she was at home she always baked cookies on Saturday morning. Aunt Hilda had asked her to make a special kind today, using the little cookie cutters which she had brought from Holland for her great-aunt.

"Why, there's a windmill," Nan remarked, as Wanda showed her the box of cutters.

"And here's our Sinterklaas," Wanda said, holding him up. "And here's his helper. I'll make a white-cookie Sinterklaas and a chocolate-cookie helper!"

Nan wanted to assist Wanda, but the Dutch girl worked so fast and so cleverly that there was nothing for Nan to do. In no time at all, there was a bowl of batter ready to be made into cookies. Wanda looked at Nan and smiled.

"Suppose you cut out the cookies," she said.

Nan had learned from Dinah how to do this. She sprinkled flour on a board, then put part of the batter on it. She sprinkled more flour over the top, then rolled the batter very thin with a rolling pin.

Next she used the cutters to make windmills, Christmas trees, and various animals. The most interesting shape was a lovely, big-eared dog, pulling a small sled.

"I hope this dog won't fall apart before I get him into the oven," Nan said, laughing.

When she picked him up, this was exactly what happened. Try as she might, Nan could not get the dog and his cart onto the cookie pan. Wanda finally showed her how, by slipping a thin knife under the batter from the nose of the dog to the back of the cart, and flipping it onto the pan.

While the cookies were baking, Wanda made the chocolate batch. Just as she finished, Aunt Hilda came in and asked if Nan had had enough cooking for one day.

"Oh, no," Nan replied. "Aren't we going to make the candy now?"

Mrs. Vandermeer thought they might as well do all their cooking that morning. Then the kitchen could be thoroughly cleaned, so that it would be bright and spotless for Sunday. She got milk, cream, sugar, vanilla, and a can of powdered chocolate. As Nan watched her mix the ingredients to make Dutch chocolate, the girl thought she was going to remember exactly how it was done. But Aunt Hilda kept tasting it and putting in a little more of this and a little more of that, until Nan was completely confused as to just how much of anything was in the mixing bowl. The only thing she knew was that there was still no chocolate in it.

Aunt Hilda had put the chocolate in a copper kettle which she had set into a larger kettle full of boiling water.

"When do you mix the chocolate in?" Nan asked.

"As soon as the chocolate is thoroughly melted," Aunt Hilda replied. "Only I don't put the chocolate into the other part. I put the other part into the chocolate. That is, after it's warm." Then she added, "You must never let this white mixture get too hot before you blend it with the chocolate, or it won't make nice, smooth candy."

Nan sighed. What a lot to remember!

Finally all the ingredients were mixed. Mrs. Vandermeer stirred constantly with a large wooden spoon. Presently she said:

"Nan, would you like to stir this while I get the cooling pans ready for the candy?"

Nan took the spoon and stirred the mixture slowly. It was not many seconds later when Freddie Bobbsey came into the kitchen and spied the two batches of cookies.

"Oh, gee! Cookies!" he burst out. "When can we eat them?"

"Shush!" his sister warned him.

As she said this, Nan turned halfway around to see that her small brother did not help himself to any of the newly baked goodies. When she turned her back to the stove, her sleeve caught in the handle of the pot of boiling chocolate candy.

In the twinkling of an eye, the big copper kettle upset. The hot candy splashed over Nan Bobbsey's arm.

CHAPTER XII

THE PRIZE FISH

NAN SCREAMED as the hot chocolate candy burned her arm. Fortunately, none of it reached her face.

Wanda and Aunt Hilda exclaimed something in Dutch. Instantly Aunt Hilda grabbed a large bottle of cooking oil and poured it on Nan's arm.

Nan had managed not to cry, but the burn pained severely. In a few minutes, however, the tingling sensation went away. She suddenly thought of the ruined candy.

"I'm dreadfully sorry," she said.

"We'll make some more," Aunt Hilda told her comfortingly. "I'm just thankful that you weren't burned worse."

All this time Freddie had been standing in a corner. He knew the accident had been partly his fault. He wished there were some way he could make up for it. Suddenly he said aloud:

"Aunt Hilda, I'm not going to eat any of these cookies."

This remark completely took Nan's mind off her own troubles. She laughed aloud and asked her small brother whatever made him decide such a thing. Freddie told her.

"Maybe if I stay out of the kitchen, it won't be so hard," he added, and ran off.

Freddie could be very good when he wanted to be. When the delicious cookies were served with dessert at the luncheon table, he did not eat any of them.

Dirk asked his aunt if he might take a bag of the cookies with him that afternoon. He and Bert were going over to the lake to try to catch some fish. All morning they had been mending a net which Uncle Pieter had brought from Holland. The loyal Hollander knew there were no finer nets in the whole world than those which Dutch fishermen make. This one had lasted a long time, but now many of the strands were broken.

Dirk was an expert at tying new pieces of string to the old ones, but after a while even he had heaved a sigh of despair. He said that it would be much easier to make a new net, so now the two boys trotted off to do this.

"I'll help you," Wanda offered, and her brother was glad to let her, since she, too, knew how to tie a fishing net.

Nan was sorry she could not help because her

arm and hand were bandaged. But Uncle Pieter offered to take her place. It seemed to Nan that it took them no time at all to finish the eight-foot-square net and attach bamboo poles to two sides of it.

"All ready," Uncle Pieter said. "I'll drive you boys over to the lake."

When they reached it, Uncle Pieter pointed. "It's very shallow near shore," he said. "You can wade out there and drag your net. I'll return for you in a couple of hours."

After removing their shoes and socks, and rolling up their trousers, Bert and Dirk grasped the poles of the net, and waded along, several feet from shore.

"Let's look now," Dirk said, a few minutes later.

The boys pulled up the net. Three little fish were splashing in it.

"Gosh!" Bert exclaimed. "They're no bigger than sardines."

He and Dirk threw the little fish back into the lake and started to drag the net again. Just then an elderly man in a rowboat pulled up near by. He smiled at the boys.

"How's luck?" he asked them.

They replied that it was bad.

"How'd you like to row with me to a place

where you might catch a big one?" he asked.

The boys thanked him and climbed in. They offered to row, and each took an oar.

"I'm trolling for muskies," the man said.

He explained that the full name of the fish was muskellunge, and that the big ones which were caught in Lake Michigan sometimes weighed as much as eighty pounds.

"We rarely find muskies weighing over ten pounds in this lake," he said. He grinned. "But ten pounds of fish will feed a lot of people."

As the boys rowed, Bert looked around at the beautiful countryside. Here and there he could see farmhouses. Around them were fields and fields of blooming tulips.

"By Monday there will be plenty of folks here," the fisherman remarked.

Bert was amazed that the man would speak aloud. Mr. Bobbsey had told his son that one must be very quiet while fishing, in order to get a nibble on the line. The boy made no reply to the man's remark.

"Sometimes," the fisherman went on, "when the tulips are in bloom, so many people come here to see them that there isn't room enough for everybody. Then the big boats that make overnight trips on Lake Michigan tie up for the week, and people sleep on them."

Since the fisherman seemed to think it was all right to talk, Bert decided to speak, too.

"I don't live around here," he said. "My family came to see the parade and everything. Our teacher told us that there are going to be some prizes this year."

"That's right. Those gold, diamond-studded klompen sure are beautiful. And there are some nice prizes for the children. There's a toy windmill I wouldn't mind owning myself."

"A windmill?" Bert asked.

He immediately thought of Freddie and his smashed toy windmill at home. Wouldn't it be wonderful if by some chance his small brother could win the windmill?

The fisherman lapsed into silence, and the boys stopped talking, too. Ten minutes went by. There was no tug on the line which the man was holding in his hand. He seemed to have forgotten his promise to take Dirk and Bert to a good fishing spot.

"Guess we may as well take it easy," he said.

With that he pulled in the line. Then he lifted up the rear seat of the boat, and took out a contraption from which hung a tiny bell. The fisherman adjusted it to the stern of the boat. Next, he threaded his line through it, and tied one end to a hook set in the bottom of the boat.

Bert smiled. He had once read about bells being used for ice fishing, but he had never heard of anyone using them this way.

He waited patiently for a muskie to tug the line and make the bell ring. The fisherman had more patience than either Dirk or Bert. After half an hour had gone by, they asked the man if he would mind taking them to the spot he had mentioned.

The fisherman looked disappointed. He had hoped to prove to these visitors that he could catch fish just as easily with homemade equipment as another person could with a fine fishing outfit. With a sigh he told the boys to turn the boat toward a certain part of the shore.

They had nearly reached it when suddenly the little bell tinkled. Instantly the three fishermen sat up straight. The man motioned for the boys to stop rowing. Very slowly he pulled the line toward him. A moment later he let some of it go out again. Then he started to pull it in once more. A grin spread over the fisherman's face.

"I think she's going to be a beauty," he said.

Bert had been fishing many times with his father and other men, as well as with boys his own age. But he had never seen anyone more clever at landing a fish than this man in the boat. Slowly he played the fish, until at last he brought it alongside the boat. Then, with a hand net, he scooped up a wonderful, big fish with a long snout.

"What did I tell you!" he cried. "I'll bet she's the biggest muskie that's been caught here this summer!"

He weighed it on a little scales he carried. The muskie was fifteen pounds.

The two boys congratulated the fisherman, and agreed with him that his strange, homemade equipment certainly had landed him a prize. As the fish flopped around in the bottom of the boat, Dirk and Bert tried their luck, but did not get a bite. Finally they asked the man to show them the spot he had mentioned earlier, where they might catch something in their net.

The boys rowed close to the shore where the fisherman pointed and hopped out of the boat. They said good-bye, and dropped the net again. Suddenly there was a big splash, sending a spray of water into Bert's face.

"We've got something big!" he shouted.

The fisherman, who was not far away, rowed back.

The boys had pulled up the net. To their utter amazement, there were several small fish in it. And among the flapping mass was a very large muskie!

The fisherman stared, then grinned.

"Well, I'll be a tulip eater!" he exclaimed. "Never saw a muskie netted so near shore before. You got a bigger one than I did!"

The two boys were thrilled with their catch, especially after the fisherman told them that at the end of each summer the person catching the largest fish during the season had his name put on a plaque that hung in the town hall.

"I'd like to bet right now," the fisherman said, "that your names will be on it this year. What you have to do now is take your muskie over to the clubhouse and let them weigh it for you."

The boys could hardly wait to get to the clubhouse, which was within walking distance. As the fisherman left them, Dirk and Bert suddenly wondered what to do with the other fish in the net.

"Maybe we ought to leave them in the water," Dirk suggested. "We can find some stakes and hammer them into the sand to hold the net. I'll look for some."

As Bert grasped the net at the edge of the water, a voice behind him said suddenly:

"You didn't expect to see me here, did you?"

Bert turned. There stood Danny Rugg!

"Where'd you come from?" Bert asked in astonishment.

"My mother and father could come out here as well as yours," Danny told Bert with a smirk.

"Sure, they can," Bert replied, but he did not say he was glad to see Danny. In fact, he was not glad to see him.

"What you got in that net?" Danny asked, pushing Bert out of his way.

"Leave that alone!" Bert cried out.

"I guess I can look if I want to," Danny insisted.

With that he grabbed one of the poles and yanked open the net. In an instant the fish were free.

As Bert looked on in horror, his prize muskie swam away!

CHAPTER XIII

NAN'S DISCOVERY

WHEN THE wonderful, big muskellunge disappeared in the lake, Bert Bobbsey was so angry that he doubled up his fist and aimed straight for Danny Rugg. The blow caught the other boy on the chest, and he toppled over into the water.

"You—you ought to stay there and never come out again!" Bert yelled.

From a distance Dirk had seen the whole thing, and came running up. He did not know who Danny was, of course, but the fact that he had been the cause of the prize fish escaping was enough for him. As Danny struggled to his feet gasping, Dirk rushed into the water and pushed him over again, crying out angrily in his own language.

Danny, dripping wet and gulping, did not fight back. Instead, he got up spluttering and slunk away.

Bert explained that Danny Rugg came from Lakeport. He related the story of the pirates' cave; how Freddie had found the missing paper dolls, and how Bert and Charlie Mason had unearthed the rest of the pirates' loot.

"I suppose Danny figured out who did it," Bert said, "and this was a good way to get square."

Dirk laughed. As the boys walked back to the place where they were to meet Uncle Pieter, Dirk told a story of what had happened one time at his school in Holland. There was a boy just about Danny's age named Jan. Once, when the whole class went on a skating party, Jan took the lunches and hid them.

"We were on a canal where we couldn't buy anything to eat, and we were nearly starved," Dirk said. "So the rest of us boys decided to play a joke on Jan."

"How did you do it?" Bert asked.

"We found out that Jan was afraid of ghosts. We thought if he ever saw one he probably would never do anything mean again."

Dirk said that a couple of the fellows got Jan to go to an old windmill, saying they had heard that a treasure was buried inside. When Jan opened the door and went in, there stood a ghost! Jan screamed and tried to back out, but the other boys held the door shut tight.

Dirk giggled. "I was the ghost," he told Bert.

"In a very low voice, I said, 'You-u-u are a b-a-a-ad boy to take the l-u-n-c-h-e-s.'

"Jan was frightened half to death. He yelled, 'I'll never do it again.'

"Then I said, 'You will be punished. You must bring chocolate for everyone at the next skating picnic.'"

Bert laughed. "And did he?"

"Yes," Dirk said. "But he didn't have enough money to buy so much chocolate, so he had to work and earn the money for it."

As the Dutch boy finished his story, they reached the spot where Mr. Vandermeer had left them. Presently he drove up. He had come for the boys early, planning to spend a little time fishing with them. When he heard the story about the prize muskie which had been lost, he felt very sorry.

Together they dragged the net hopefully, then tried fishing with a pole. Finally Uncle Pieter caught a small muskie.

They drove home in time to have some of the fish cooked for supper. It tasted delicious, but all the time Bert was eating he could not get the thought of Danny and the prize muskie out of his mind.

It was not until later, when he heard that Miss Vandermeer had signed up all the children for the Children's Parade, that Bert forgot about the big fish. He decided that perhaps, instead of wearing one of Dirk's good-looking costumes, he would put on old clothes and go as a Dutch fisherman. He borrowed some from Uncle Pieter, and his mother said she would fix them so they would fit Bert.

Aunt Hilda already had started work on costumes for Freddie and Flossie. From a trunk she had taken out some clothes brought from Holland. Aunt Hilda was sure she never would wear them again, since they were now too small for her.

From one dress she had cut a quaint little outfit for Flossie. It was now basted together and ready to be tried on. When Nan saw her little sister, she exclaimed:

"Oh, Flossie, you look so cute! You look just like one of those big Dutch dolls that we see at Christmastime."

It was true that Flossie did look very cunning. Her blonde curls and blue eyes and dimples made her a picture under the little lace bonnet.

"Only I'm a talking doll," she said. Turning to Aunt Hilda, she asked, "Will it be all right if I talk in the parade?"

Aunt Hilda thought for a moment, then said she believed it might be better if Flossie really pretended to be a doll. "Can you walk like one?"

Flossie turned her head slightly to one side, raised her arms from the elbows, and stepped jerkily across the floor.

Aunt Hilda laughed. "That's perfect," she said. "Do it just that way in the parade, and I believe you might win a prize."

Freddie had come in to see what was going on. He was just in time to hear the last remark, and told himself he would like to win a prize, too.

"Did you make me a suit?" he asked his kindly hostess.

"No, I haven't started yet."

Freddie said he thought instead of wearing a suit, he would like to be a windmill.

Flossie giggled. "You only have two arms," she told her twin. "Where are you going to get two more?"

Freddie had not thought of this, but he was sure the problem could be solved. What was more important was whether a costume could be made for him so that he would look like a windmill.

"I could look out through a window in it," he told Aunt Hilda. "Then I wouldn't fall down."

Mrs. Vandermeer was intrigued by the idea, and said that on Monday she would figure out something so the little boy could have his wish.

The next day was Sunday and at Tulip Land Farm, all work and play ceased.

Flossie frowned. "Don't you even feed the cows?" she asked.

Mrs. Vandermeer said yes, indeed, they fed the cows and the chickens and the cats, but that was all the work they did.

"I hope you don't mind," she said to all of them in the room, "but on Sunday we eat only cold food. No cooking is done here on Sunday." She went on to say that everyone who lived at Tulip Land Farm always went to church. Anyone who happened to be visiting was invited to go, too.

"Just the way we did in Holland," Aunt Hilda concluded.

Since the Bobbseys always attended church when they were at home, they were very glad to go the following day. On the way home from service, Uncle Pieter drove them through the town where the Tulpen Feest parade was to be held. Stores and public buildings were already decorated for the festive occasion.

But this did not interest the Bobbsey twins and the children from Holland so much as the prizes, which were on display in a department-store window. When Freddie spied the toy windmill to be given away, he gave a low whistle.

"That's super!" he said. "Don't you think so, Bert?"

Bert agreed and also Dirk. Even the girls thought it would be a fine toy to own, although they liked the beautiful dolls better, especially the one which was marked *The Princess*.

Mrs. Bobbsey exclaimed over the golden, diamond-studded klompen which stood in the center of the display of prizes. Anyone would be delighted to own such beautiful and valuable little shoes.

The visitors walked on, and had just come to a corner, when Nan suddenly caught her breath. She grabbed Miss Vandermeer's hand.

"Look!" she cried. "The man just going down that street. He looked like Mr. Sam Tomson!"

"Really?"

The teacher was dumfounded. What would Sam Tomson be doing in Tulip Land?

The instant Bert heard the name Tomson, he raced across the street after the man they thought had stolen Miss Vandermeer's rare old book of pictures. Before the boy had gone far, Uncle Pieter shouted:

"Stop!"

Bert stopped running and turned around. Uncle Pieter told him that on Sunday it was not the custom to race through the streets.

"But, Uncle Pieter," Miss Vandermeer spoke up, "we think that man is a thief."

"Well, that's different," Mr. Vandermeer conceded. "Go get him, Bert!"

Mr. Vandermeer himself started to run, but by this time the other man was out of sight. If he was Sam Tomson, he must have seen Nan and Bert and the teacher. He had made his escape.

Uncle Pieter and his family were told the whole story. They were shocked to hear about the stolen book. Aunt Hilda remembered it well, and described it in detail to Dirk and Wanda.

"It's a great loss," she told them. "Whoever took the book could sell it for a lot of money."

Miss Vandermeer said she was puzzled as to why Sam Tomson should have come to Michigan. Nan suggested that this would be a good place in which to sell the book. So many of the people who lived here were interested in Holland that they probably would be delighted to have such a fine collection of Dutch pictures.

"That's certainly a very good explanation," Miss Vandermeer said.

"I'm sure you're right, Nan," Uncle Pieter agreed. "I believe we should stop and tell the police you suspect that the thief is in town, before he has a chance to sell the book. Let's do it right now!"

CHAPTER XIV

FREDDIE IN THE SAND

AFTER the police had been told about Sam Tomson, the Bobbseys and the Vandermeers went home.

A cold dinner was set on the big dining-room table in the Vandermeer farmhouse. Everyone was to help himself, and was expected to wash and dry whatever dishes and silver he used, and to put them away.

Freddie Bobbsey looked at all the good food. He took a slice of ham and a chicken leg. The little boy quickly passed by the pickles, the heaped-up cottage cheese, and a platter of cole-slaw. He hurried to a large silver basket filled with cookies, which he had spied across the table. Freddie's punishment of himself had ended. Now he could eat as many cookies as he wished!

Freddie filled his plate with white and choco-late Christmas trees, Sinterklaases, and dogcarts. A few minutes later, when his mother found him sitting in a corner like Little Jack Horner, she gasped.

"My goodness, Freddie," she said, "you have enough cookies here for three days. How about saving some for tomorrow and the next day?"

The small boy looked up at her. "Mother," he said, "I promise not to eat too many, but will you please let me eat them till I can't eat any more?"

Mrs. Bobbsey frowned. Freddie's reasoning was certainly strange! She told him he might not know until too late whether or not he had over-eaten. "And remember, Freddie," she added, "if you make yourself ill, you won't be able to go in the Children's Parade."

That settled it. Without another word, Freddie handed all but three cookies to his mother. It meant more to him to try winning the toy windmill than it did to eat the Dutch cakes.

"But it's funny about those cookies," he thought. "Every time I start to eat them, something happens."

That afternoon Uncle Pieter said he would like to drive his visitors along the lake shore to see the sand dunes. He told the children that many, many years before, when the people from Holland had come to the United States looking for a place to settle, these sand dunes had reminded them of their own country. So they had stayed here.

When the Bobbseys reached the dunes, the wind was blowing hard. Even though the tall grass kept the sand from being carried away, still there was plenty of it swirling around.

"It's almost like a snowstorm," Nan remarked.

"It hurts my face and gets in my eyes," Flossie said. She closed her eyes and let Nan lead her.

Uncle Pieter was striding toward the water, the rest following. He did not seem to mind the sand.

As the wind grew stronger, Freddie could hardly walk. Finally he turned his back to the wind and tried to walk backward. This made him fall behind the others.

Deciding it would be fun to climb the dune, the little boy started up. At the top, he called to the others, but the wind carried his voice away from them. The blowing sand swished into his eyes so that he had to close them tight.

Suddenly he lost his balance and toppled down the side of the dune. A shower of sand covered all but his head.

Freddie fought to get up, but the sliding sand kept pressing down upon him. He became frightened.

Down at the shore of the lake, Mrs. Bobbsey

suddenly missed her small son. She looked around quickly. Then, not seeing him, she rushed back toward the automobile.

On the way she kept calling Freddie's name. Mrs. Bobbsey could not understand why he did not answer. Suddenly she saw a heaving movement in the sand, on the side of one of the dunes.

She rushed over to the spot and pulled the struggling child to his feet. Freddie coughed and blinked, but after a few moments he felt all right.

By this time, the other Bobbsey children had begun to wonder where Freddie was. Their mother, too, had disappeared. So the whole group went back to the car. Mrs. Bobbsey and Freddie were inside.

"I didn't mean to do something so soon again," Freddie apologized, "but the sand just came up and hit me."

After Uncle Pieter heard that the wind and sand were bothering Flossie and Freddie, he said, "I'm so used to working in the tulip fields, I guess my old face is pretty tough."

Freddie smiled. "I think I'll stay outdoors all the time and get my face tough, so I won't have to shut my eyes in the wind," he said. "It's just a sissy face now."

"You'd better not let Danny Rugg hear you say that," Bert advised.

"Where do you suppose Danny's staying?" Nan asked her twin.

Bert said he hoped it was so far away that he would not see him again during their stay in Tulip Land. But they had barely reached home when a car drove up to the door.

To the amazement of the Bobbsey twins, Mr. and Mrs. Rugg and Danny got out. They were as surprised to see the Bobbseys as the Bobbseys were to see them. Mr. Rugg explained that his wife wanted to buy some bulbs for black tulips, and had been told that Mr. Vandermeer had the best bulbs in the area.

"And he does, too," Freddie spoke up proudly.

The tulip farmer smiled at Freddie's loyalty. Turning to Mr. Rugg, he said:

"I'm sorry, but I make it a rule never to transact business on Sunday. If you'll come back tomorrow, I'll be glad to sell you some bulbs. In the meantime, look around if you care to."

Danny did not wait for his father to answer. He started off at once to inspect the farm.

To keep him from doing anything mischievous, Dirk and Bert caught up with Danny. They were just in time to stop him from picking some of the tulips.

"You can't get away with that a second time!" Bert shouted at him.

"What do you mean?" Danny demanded.

"You know what I mean, all right," Bert told him. "You picked Nan's tulips and took them to school."

"I told you before, I didn't take them," Danny said, but this time he did not look Bert in the eye.

Bert introduced Dirk to Danny. The Bobbsey boy winked at Dirk and said:

"Do you know what happens to boys who play tricks in Holland, Danny?"

"No," the boy replied. "What?"

With a solemn face, Dirk retold the story about the ghost in the windmill, only he did not say that he had been the ghost. He let Danny think that a real ghost had come to frighten the Dutch boy Jan.

While Dirk was telling the story, Bert kept looking off into space and smiling. Danny followed the line of his gaze. Bert was looking straight at the windmill on Tulip Land Farm!

Danny understood what Bert meant. He had been planning to go inside the old windmill, but now he guessed he would not take a chance on meeting a ghost! In fact, he decided, it might be just as well to leave the island before Bert and Dirk got square with him for letting their prize fish escape.

At this moment Freddie came running up.

"Hi, Danny!" he said. "I'm going to be a windmill in the Children's Parade!"

"The Children's Parade?" Danny asked. "Oh, that."

He smiled rather a crooked smile, like the one Bert had seen on Sam Tomson's face.

"You aren't going to be *anything* in the Children's Parade, Freddie," Danny said.

"Why not?" Freddie asked hotly.

"Why, didn't you know?" Danny said gleefully. "Only children who live here all the time can be in the parade."

CHAPTER XV

THE FUNNY COSTUME

DANNY laughed, as Freddie stared unbelievingly. He could not be in the Children's Parade!

"Are you sure, Danny?" he asked.

"Yes."

A woman's voice called, "Danny! Danny! Where are you?" It was the boy's mother.

"How'd you find out about the Children's Parade?" Bert asked him.

Danny did not answer. He was enjoying the dismay on the other boys' faces.

"Danny!" his father shouted.

Danny finally went to the Rugg car where his parents were waiting. They had told Mr. Vandermeer that they would come back to buy some black tulip bulbs before they returned to Lakeport.

After Mr. Rugg had driven off with his wife and son, Freddie ran up to his mother. He looked very sad.

"Mother," he said, trying to hold back his

tears, "Danny said we can't be in the Children's Parade!"

Mrs. Bobbsey and the other grownups who stood near by were amazed to hear this. They asked how Danny had found out. Freddie said the boy had not told him.

"It's probably true," Bert said. "I'll bet Danny tried to sign up for the parade and couldn't do it because he doesn't live here."

Uncle Pieter and Aunt Hilda were very sorry to hear of this ruling about the Children's Parade. All their young visitors had been looking forward to the event. Personally, Uncle Pieter did not see why outsiders could not join in the festivities as well as the local children, and said so.

"Maybe it has something to do with costumes," Nan spoke up.

"In what way?" Miss Vandermeer asked.

Nan thought that perhaps the costumes worn in the parade had to belong to the children who wore them. Since it was unlikely that anyone visiting in Tulip Land would own a Dutch costume, maybe visitors would not be allowed to parade.

"I hardly think the Tulpen Feest committee would decide such a thing," the teacher remarked. "Everyone in this area is so friendly and anxious to see the visitors have a good time. I doubt if they would do anything to hurt people's feelings."

The matter remained a mystery, and the Bobbsey twins and Dirk and Wanda went to bed that night feeling very sad over the turn of events. To look at the parade would be fun, of course, but taking part in it would have been much more exciting.

When they assembled at the breakfast table the following morning, Miss Vandermeer was not there. Her aunt said she had driven to town early.

"My niece didn't say why she went," Aunt Hilda told the children, "but I have an idea."

"What is it?" Flossie and Freddie asked together.

Aunt Hilda suggested that they guess, but none of them could think of any good reason. They thought perhaps she wanted to look at the schools, but Aunt Hilda said these were not open today. The local children were having a holiday.

"Just like us," Freddie said. "I wonder how our old school is getting along?"

Flossie, putting down the spoon with which she was eating her oatmeal, said, "I wonder if they got all the shakes out of the building."

Uncle Pieter Vandermeer asked what she meant. The little girl explained that the earthquake had made the school shake until it got weak.

"Maybe I should have said, 'I wonder if they got all the weaks out of it,'" Flossie added.

The others laughed. Mrs. Bobbsey remarked that the carpenters and bricklayers and plumbers and electricians who were working on the building would be surprised to hear that they had been hired to get all the shakes and "weaks" out of the building.

"Just the same, I hope they do," Uncle Pieter said, a twinkle in his eye. "It would be funny to sit in a schoolhouse that couldn't stand still!"

As they finished breakfast, Miss Vandermeer drove up and came in. When she said good morning to the children, the teacher smiled.

"No more worries," she said. "Everything's fixed up for the parade."

"You mean—you mean we can be in it?" Freddie shouted.

"I mean exactly that," Miss Vandermeer answered. "I went directly to the chairman of the Tulpen Feest committee and told him our story. He said he did not know why anyone would have told Danny that children who are visiting could not be in the parade."

"Then Danny must have made it up," Bert declared.

The other children were too excited about the good news to care whether or not Danny had made up the story.

"Freddie, I have a surprise for you," the teacher said, handing him a package she was carrying.

"May I open it right away?" the little boy asked.

"Oh, please do."

Freddie had a little trouble getting the string off, but finally he managed to unwrap the package. Inside was some dark-brown muslin. He looked up at Miss Vandermeer, puzzled. Her eyes were dancing.

"Guess what it's for," she suggested.

Freddie could not figure it out. When he told the teacher this, she said:

"There's another bundle out in the car. Bert, suppose you bring it in."

Upon seeing the bundle, Freddie was more puzzled than ever. There was a quantity of thin, weathered, house shingles. Tied with them were several strips of narrow wood. Suddenly it dawned on the little boy what was to be done with this queer assortment of things.

"My windmill costume!" he shouted gleefully.

"I'll give you a high mark," the teacher said, laughing. "You've guessed right."

None of the children could imagine how the costume was to be made, so Miss Vandermeer explained that first they would build a sort of rack to cover Freddie's body. At the top would be a small hoop to sit on his head, and there would be a large one just above his feet. The thin pieces of wood could be nailed to the hoops, and over these would be fastened the brown muslin.

"Then will come the hard part," the teacher said. "The shingles will have to be fastened to the cloth with tacks. Then someone will have to hammer the points flat on the other side."

Everyone worked on the windmill suit. Dirk made the hoops. Bert tacked on the stays to hold them together. At this point, Freddie decided to try on the frame. Flossie started to giggle.

"You look like a monkey in a cage," she said.

"It's such a beautiful morning," Miss Vandermeer said presently, "that we should all be outdoors. How about a trip into the tulip fields to see what the men are doing?"

She led the way to where Uncle Pieter was busy inspecting his flowers.

"How many kinds of tulips are there?" Freddie asked him.

"Well, son, I'd say there are over a thousand different varieties."

This figure was far beyond anything Freddie

could imagine, so Mr. Vandermeer said to him:

"Think of it this way. You know how long it took you to come here from home in the airplane, and you know how fast it went. Well, if you should drop a different kind of tulip every half mile, all the way from here to Lakeport, you still would have one left to plant in your own garden!"

"Wowee!" said Freddie, and thought what fun it would be to try such a thing.

He and Flossie decided to go back to the island and play, so they trotted off.

In the meantime, the others went farther into the fields. Nan asked the tulip farmer how deep he planted his bulbs. She was sure the ones she had planted in her garden had not been right, because the stems were much shorter and the flowers only one-third the size of the Vandermeer tulips.

"It all depends on what kind of soil you have," he answered. "If the earth is light and sandy, you dig a hole three times the size of the bulb and plant it. But you must never make it hard for the little shoots to come up through heavy soil, so they shouldn't be planted deeper than two and a half times their size, if they're being put into heavy, clay soil."

Miss Vandermeer asked Dirk and Wanda if they knew where tulips had come from originally. They smiled and said that they had learned this in school.

"Tulips first grew wild in Turkey," Dirk replied, "and their name was *Tülbend*. That's also the Turkish word for turban."

"A tulip does look like a turban turned upside down," Nan remarked. "I never thought of that."

She had barely spoken when a deep-toned bell sounded loudly.

"The dinner bell," Miss Vandermeer explained.

Instead of ringing once, however, the big bell kept on with a loud *bong, bong*. Uncle Pieter, who had been digging out a bulb, straightened up. Then he started to run.

"That's the fire bell!" he exclaimed.

CHAPTER XVI

A MUD PIE MISBEHAVES

AS THE tulip farmer sped toward his home, the children hurried after him, followed by Miss Vandermeer. Each one wondered what was on fire. Was it the house, or one of the barns?

The boys outdistanced the others. As they reached the bridge, they saw Flossie and Freddie coming out of the barn. The twins were pulling a small hose cart.

"Where's the fire?" Bert shouted. Then he noticed that a lot of the living-room furniture was on the lawn. "The fire must be in there!" he told Dirk.

The two of them rushed into the living room. No one was there. And nothing was on fire.

They raced outside again. Freddie and Flossie were just disappearing behind the house. Bert and Dirk grabbed the hose cart.

"Hey, leave that alone!" Freddie yelled. "This is our fire!"

"Your fire?" Bert asked. "What do you mean?"

Freddie pointed. A thin wisp of smoke was curling from the doorway of a shed back of the house. As the children ran forward, an old Dutchman appeared. He was puffing on a long clay pipe.

"Is the fire bad?" Freddie cried out.

"Fire?" the old man asked. "Far as I know, the only fire around here is in my pipe."

"You m-mean the shed's not on fire?" Fireman Freddie demanded.

The man, who worked for Mr. Vandermeer, scratched his head, perplexed. Then he smiled.

"I guess you saw the smoke from my pipe coming out the door."

Freddie was dreadfully disappointed to learn that there was no fire for him to put out. But Uncle Pieter and the others, arriving, were relieved. They were still puzzled about the fire bell.

"Who rang that?" Nan asked.

Flossie giggled. "I did. Aunt Hilda told me to ring it."

"Aunt Hilda?" Dirk said in surprise. "Why would she—"

At this moment Aunt Hilda herself came out the shed door. She laughed heartily when she heard about Freddie and Flossie's mistake.

"But I'm glad you're on the job," she said,

"even when it comes to ringing the fire alarm."

It was Flossie's turn to look surprised. Mrs. Vandermeer had asked her to ring the big bell out in the garden, to summon everyone to lunch. The little girl had thought it fun to keep on ringing the bell, never dreaming that it meant a fire alarm.

And it was directly afterward that Freddie had seen the smoke. Knowing where the hose cart was, he had called to Flossie to help him.

"What about the furniture on the lawn?" asked Bert. "That had nothing to do with a fire?"

"No," Aunt Hilda answered. "This is one of our cleaning days. I follow the custom of Dutch housewives, and air as much of our furniture as we can carry outside when we clean."

She said that it was easier to clean her rooms with no furniture in them; at the same time the pure, fresh outside air was getting into her cushions and pillows and rugs.

"When they come back inside," Flossie spoke up, "they bring all the fresh air with them, don't they?"

"They do indeed," Mrs. Vandermeer replied. "And it makes the house smell sweet and fresh."

Aunt Hilda told the children that luncheon today would be a picnic. She asked Wanda and

Dirk, who had been there longer and knew where things were, to get out the picnic table and benches. Nan and Bert helped them cart the rustic outfit from the shed. The table was set up on the grass among the tulip gardens, and Nan thought she had never seen a lovelier spot for a picnic.

Mrs. Vandermeer and the woman who helped her keep the house clean set the food on the long table. The first course was steaming pea soup with pork sausage in it. After the Bobbsey family had tasted the delicious soup, the twins' mother asked Mrs. Vandermeer for the recipe so that Dinah might make it for them at home.

The next course was a special kind of hot pastry. Wanda told the Bobbseys the little cakes were called *poffertjes*. They were about the size of a fifty-cent piece, and were made of buckwheat meal.

The Bobbseys watched to see what Wanda and Dirk would do with them. The two Dutch children put a big pat of butter in the center. As soon as this melted, they sprinkled on powdered sugar from a wooden shaker.

"Gee! This is good!" Bert exclaimed after eating one. "I could eat three or four of these!"

Wanda laughed. She said that at the big fairs in Holland people had what they called a *poffertjes-eten*. This meant that they all ate just as many of the little pastries as they could hold.

"One time, I ate twenty-four," Dirk told them.

"Wow!" cried Freddie, who already had lost his appetite. The big dish of soup had nearly filled him up.

The Bobbsey twins did not come anywhere near eating twenty-four poffertjes apiece. Bert managed ten of them, but Nan, who had spied the dessert, decided to stop after eating six.

When the children had finished the dessert of pudding topped with jelly, Freddie and Flossie asked what they might do next.

"Please stay around the house, Freddie," Aunt Hilda said. "I want to try on your windmill suit. Most of the shingles are on it now."

Wanda asked the small twins how they would like to play a marketing game.

"How do you do that?" Freddie wanted to know. He thought it sounded pretty good.

The Dutch girl explained that in Holland, instead of women going to the markets, the grocers and butchers came to their homes.

"The women who live in second-floor apartments don't like to come downstairs, and the merchants don't like to go up," Wanda continued, giggling.

"They might bring in mud," Aunt Hilda put

in, laughing. "And Dutch housewives do not like dirt in their homes."

"So what do they do?" Flossie asked.

Wanda said that they used a basket tied to a long rope. The grocer put the articles into the basket, and the housewife pulled it up. Then she would put the money into it, and let the basket down.

"Oh, what fun!" Flossie said, clapping her hands. "Let's play that game!"

Dirk found a piece of clothesline and tied one end of it to the leg of a chair in Flossie's bedroom. The little girl dropped the line out the window. To the end of it, Wanda tied a market basket which Aunt Hilda gave her.

"I guess you won't need us any longer," Wanda said. "Nan and Bert, let's go for a bicycle ride."

"Oh, that will be fun," Nan exclaimed.

When the older children left, Freddie went to the kitchen to borrow some packages of rice and prunes and oatmeal. After Flossie had pulled these up three times in the basket, and sent down some leaves for play money, the twins grew tired of these grocery packages.

"Let's make some things to play with," Freddie called up to his sister.

"Like what?" she asked, leaning out the window.

Once, when Freddie was in Mexico, he had gone to an Indian market. He remembered how the women had made pancakes and salads to sell to the people going by.

"Let's make mud pies with greens on top," he suggested.

Flossie thought that this was a fine idea, and ran downstairs to help her twin. The two children worked for several minutes making the mud pies. Freddie broke off some blades of grass and laid them across the pies.

In the meantime, Flossie had asked Aunt Hilda if she might have a few flowers. Since tulips would be too large to decorate the pies with, Mrs. Vandermeer told her where there were some blue and white violets growing. The little girl picked several, and ran back to put them on the mud pies.

"Oh, they look be-yootiful!" Flossie exclaimed.

She dashed up the stairs and called out the window, "What are you selling today, Mr. Marketman?"

"I have very nice chocolate pies," Freddie replied. "How many would you like?"

"How big are they?" Flossie called down.

The marketman laughed. "They're very small. I could eat all of them myself."

For a second Flossie forgot that they were playing a game. As she looked down at the mud pies, she started to giggle. Imagine Freddie eating six mud pies all at once!

Then she became serious once more, and told the marketman to send up four chocolate pies. Freddie placed them in the basket and the little girl slowly drew them up to the window. But just before it reached the sill, her fingers slipped. The basket hit the side of the house and turned part way over.

One of the mud pies flew out. Before Flossie could warn her twin, who was not looking up, the mud pie landed squarely on the top of his head!

"Golly!" Freddie cried out, as the mud ran down his face and neck.

He tried to remove it, but that only made matters worse. The mud soiled his sweater as well as his hands.

"Oh, I'm so sorry," Flossie called down from the window.

Freddie was afraid his mother would see what had happened and give him a shampoo. He wanted to avoid this if possible.

"I know what I'll do," he thought. "I'll stick my head in the canal."

Since the canal was not very deep, and Freddie

could swim, he had not been told to stay away from it. By the time Flossie got downstairs, he was already on his way to the water. Flossie caught up to him.

"Where you going?" she asked.

Her twin told her, and she had to admit that his idea was not a bad one. She suggested that he take off his sweater and let her wipe the mud from it, while he was washing his hair.

When they reached the canal, Flossie sat down on the grass. Freddie pulled off his sweater, and she shook it hard. Then she began wiping it on the clean green grass beside her.

In the meantime, Freddie had sprawled on his stomach with his arms in the water. Getting the mud out of his hair was harder than he had thought.

"I ought to have some soap," he said.

Flossie offered to go back to the house and get some, but Freddie would not let her. Mrs. Bobbsey would be sure to find out what was going on and give him the shampoo!

In order to get his hair wet, Freddie had to pull himself nearer the water. Finally he got all the mud off the top of his head, but there was no way to wash the back of it.

"Turn over on your back," Flossie suggested, "and I'll do it for you."

Her twin flopped over, and she crouched down. "You'll have to get closer to the water," she told him.

Freddie inched himself along the ground. But, unfortunately, he inched himself too far. Suddenly he took an unexpected somersault and landed in the water.

As if this were not bad enough, he pulled Flossie along with him. With a big splash, she, too, fell into the canal!

CHAPTER XVII

A STRANGE RIDE

THINKING Freddie was just outside the house, his mother called him to try on his windmill costume. When her small son did not answer, she went outside to get him. The little boy was nowhere in sight. She called him again.

Flossie, who was now standing up in the shallow canal, heard her mother's voice.

"Mother's calling, Freddie," she remarked. "We'd better go."

Freddie had nothing to say. He certainly had made a fine mess of everything, when all he had intended to do was to wash the mud off his hair.

"Come on, Freddie," Flossie urged.

The twins climbed out of the water and walked toward the house. Mrs. Bobbsey met them halfway there.

"What in the world have you been doing?" she asked. "You're both soaking wet!"

"It's all my fault," Flossie said, and told how she had dropped a mud pie on Freddie's head.

Their mother took each of them by a hand and led them to the house. Her only remark was that if many more things happened the small twins would have to stay in bed for lack of clean clothes.

"But I won't need regular clothes for the parade," Freddie replied. "And maybe I could wear my costume all the time."

Mrs. Bobbsey smiled. She told Freddie that after he tried on his windmill suit he probably would change his mind. Freddie wondered why she had said that. It ought to be fun being a little house walking around. But after he was dressed in dry clothes once more, and went downstairs to try on the suit, he knew what his mother meant.

The windmill was rather heavy and not very comfortable hanging from the little boy's head. When he said that it hurt, Aunt Hilda put a cap on his head under the hoop. Freddie declared that now he could wear the costume a long time.

"When are we going to put the arms on?" he asked.

"Right now," Aunt Hilda told him.

She picked up from the table what looked like two sets of airplane wings and fastened them to a shingle over Freddie's chest. The crossed wings reached from above his head to just below his knees.

To Freddie's delight, there was a little gadget

inside the costume that twirled the wings. He immediately began to do this.

"Oh, it's the best windmill in Tulip Land!" Freddie exclaimed. Flossie thought so, too.

Aunt Hilda led Freddie to a long mirror, and the little boy gazed at himself gleefully through the little window in the suit.

"May I take this home when we leave?" he asked Mrs. Vandermeer eagerly.

Mrs. Bobbsey answered his question by saying she did not see how they could carry such a big thing in the airplane. A look of disappointment crossed Freddie's face.

"Suppose I send it to you," Aunt Hilda offered kindly, and at once Freddie felt better.

He could hardly wait for the time of the Children's Parade to come. It was still two days off. Flossie put on her Dutch doll costume, and the two children went outside to practice how they would walk in the parade.

"I wish Nan and Bert would come home to see us," Flossie said.

But Nan and Bert were some distance from the farmhouse. They had gone on bicycles with Dirk and Wanda to do an errand for Aunt Hilda at the Boven farm.

Mr. Boven, a man who worked at Tulip Land Farm, lived about two miles away. Aunt Hilda was sending his wife a gift for her new grand-daughter in Holland.

The couple's quaint, one-story house was built of stone. Tulip gardens surrounded it.

The big front door was framed with beautiful brown tiles. On each one there was a picture of something to do with farm life. A little girl was feeding baby chicks. A boy was milking a cow. A man was bringing in hay, and a woman was making cheese.

Mrs. Boven came to the door. Wanda spoke to her in Dutch, and the woman smiled broadly at the sound of her native language.

"Welkom!" she said, and motioned for the children to come inside.

The twins heard the word "Bobbsey" and knew that they were being introduced. They were just beginning to wonder whether Mrs. Boven spoke only Dutch, when she said in English that she was very glad to meet the children from Lakeport.

"And it's also very nice to have children from Holland come to see me," she said, putting her arms around Dirk and Wanda.

Though the Boven home was small, Nan thought it was fascinating. Little blue tiles were set across the fireplace and around the window frames, and there were tables with tops made of tiles also. Mrs. Boven said that each group told a story.

The tiles over the fireplace were a series of Noah's Ark pictures. Noah himself, holding a white dove in one hand, was in the center of the group. Around him were leopards, lions, elephants, and giraffes peeking from the windows in the ark.

While explaining various other pictures, Mrs. Boven told her visitors she made tiles to order. Instantly Nan had an idea.

"I'd like to order some for my mother's birthday," she said, "if they don't cost too much."

"Well, suppose you decide," Mrs. Boven replied, and led the children to a little shed in back of the house. "This is where I make and bake my tiles," she said. "I'll show you some samples."

Nan and Bert looked at flower patterns, dancing figures, and animals of all sorts. None of them seemed to strike their fancy exactly.

Presently Nan's eyes lighted up. "Could you make tiles with children on them?" she asked.

Mrs. Boven thought she could, so Nan explained her idea. She would like four tiles, each one representing a Bobbsey twin in the Children's Parade. Mrs. Boven thought it would not be hard to make Nan as a Dutch girl, Flossie as a Dutch doll, and Bert as a Dutch fisherman.

"But trying to make your little brother look like a windmill, or make a windmill look like him, will be a real job," Mrs. Boven said, laughing. "But I'll do the best I can and not charge you much."

Since she could not finish the tiles before the twins would be leaving Tulip Land, it was arranged that she would send them to arrive on Mrs. Bobbsey's birthday.

Before leaving the interesting Boven home, the children were served hot chocolate and delicious little decorated tarts. The twins learned they were called *taartjes*. Then the children got on their bicycles and rode back to Tulip Land Farm.

There was still an hour left before suppertime, so Bert asked Dirk to stop at the windmill. The Bobbsey boy wanted to know how the wings worked. As they approached, Bert noticed the wings were not in motion. He asked Dirk why. The Dutch boy said the gears probably were locked, because the windmill was not used for farm work very often.

"You know how to make the wings go around, don't you, Dirk?" Bert asked him.

"Sure."

Since Nan wanted to see them go around, too, she and Wanda lingered on the outside of the building, while the two boys went inside.

Bert followed Dirk up a winding stairway. Presently they came to a door leading to a cat-walk which girdled the fat building. Bert peeked out. What a fine view of the tulip fields!

"Come on," Dirk said, tugging at Bert's arm. "We've got to go much higher."

Together the boys climbed until the stairs ended at a platform near the top of the windmill.

"How does this thing work?" Bert asked.

Dirk pointed to a long horizontal rod extending through the side of the windmill. "That goes to the wings," he said. "When they go round and round, the rod turns."

"Then what happens?"

Dirk looked very serious. He knew all about windmills and was proud to tell an American boy how they operated.

"The rod turns the gear right here in the center of the *molen*—I mean the windmill," Dirk said, "and that makes this shaft turn."

Bert looked at the shaft to which Dirk was pointing. It ran from the gear straight down through the inside of the building and connected with some machinery on the floor.

"I'd like to shinny down that shaft," Bert said with a grin.

Dirk frowned. "What does shinny mean?"

The Bobbsey boy laughingly told him what shinny meant and Dirk smiled.

"That would be fun," he admitted, "like riding around on the wings."

"Can you do that?"

"Oh, no," Dirk replied. "Every Dutch boy would like to, but you'd fall off. Besides, nobody's allowed to play on a windmill."

Dirk then told Bert how the shaft turned the machinery at the bottom of the windmill, providing power to grind flour and pump water.

"Gee, I'd like to see it all in operation," Bert exclaimed.

"I'll try to unlock the gears," the Dutch boy volunteered. "The wind is blowing right on the wings. You go down to the catwalk and watch them go around."

Bert hurried down the stairs and onto the catwalk. One of the big wings was right in front of him. It extended several feet down past the place where Bert was standing, and was close enough to touch.

The boy noticed that the wing had slats like an old-fashioned shutter. They were partly open.

Wanting to know what they were for, Bert ran back upstairs to ask Dirk.

"Those are to let the wind through," Dirk said, looking up from the gear on which he was tinkering.

"Why?"

"Because in a strong breeze the wings would turn too fast and break the machinery," Dirk said.

"Most of the slats are open now," Bert said. "Just a couple on one wing are shut. So we're all set."

"I'm afraid not," Dirk said sadly. "I can't get this gear unlocked. You go to the catwalk and try to open those slats. If I get this gear working, I'll call you."

Back on the catwalk, Bert stood on the railing and tried to reach the closed slats. But even on tiptoes, he was too far below to reach them. There was only one thing to do; climb up. Bert grasped the wing with his hands and swung himself onto it. Then he started to climb, using the open slats as a ladder.

He stopped for a moment and took a deep breath of fresh air, at the same time looking down at the girls. Nan and Wanda seemed like toy children, so many feet below.

They waved, but Bert could not let go to wave back. Then Nan's voice came up to him.

"Be careful, Bert!"

The boy kept on climbing. The sound of the wind and the view below made him feel like a sailor clambering high in the rigging of a sailing ship.

Finally Bert reached the closed slats and started to push them open. At the same time, inside the windmill, Dirk got the gears unlocked.

"Here they go!" he shouted. "Watch out below!"

But the wind, whistling through the slats of the windmill, drowned out Dirk's warning. As Bert clung to the big wing, it started moving.

"Help! Help!" Bert cried as he was lifted into the sky.

Nan and Wanda, looking up from below, screamed.

CHAPTER XVIII

A CHASE

BY THIS TIME, Bert, clinging desperately with both hands and feet to the shutters of the big blade, was standing upside down.

It seemed like only a second before the boy had made a complete circle. Nan, just starting to breathe a sigh of relief because she thought he could jump off onto the catwalk, gasped again.

Her brother was starting up into the air a second time!

"Oh, Bert!" she cried out.

Wanda, fearful that the boy would not be able to stick on much longer, raced inside the windmill, and cried out in Dutch:

"Bertus hangt aan een wiek!"

Dirk was horrified. Bert hanging on one of the wings! Instantly he rushed outside onto the catwalk. He tried to help Bert off as the wing came past, but could not reach him.

Wanda had dashed up the steps. She joined her brother.

"Can't you stop it?" she screamed.

"I'll lock the gears again," Dirk replied, racing to the top of the windmill. By this time Bert was on his fifth trip around.

He had clung to the shutters as tightly as he could. When Dirk locked the gears, the sudden jar nearly made Bert lose his hold on the wing. Luckily it came to a halt in front of the catwalk.

Trembling and dizzy, the boy let himself down to the catwalk, and held onto the railing. His knees were so wobbly that he could hardly stand up. Dirk and Wanda rushed down to him.

"Gee—thanks," Bert said. "I—I couldn't have held on much longer."

Dirk sighed in relief. Then he grinned. "Riding the wing is something I've always wanted to do," he said. "But I never had the nerve."

The three children joined Nan at the foot of the windmill. Then they all went to the farmhouse.

"There was somebody here to see you," Mrs. Bobbsey said, as they entered.

"To see us?" Nan and Bert asked together. "Who?"

"Your friend Danny Rugg."

Freddie told the older twins that while Mrs. Rugg was buying some black tulips he had talked to Danny about the Children's Parade, saying the

Bobbseys were going to be in it after all. Danny had become envious and asked Miss Vandermeer if she could get him in the parade, too.

"So I said I would," the teacher spoke up. "I even offered to get a costume for him."

"One of mine?" Dirk asked her. He did not like the idea of lending clothes to anyone who caused as much trouble as Danny had.

"Oh, no," Miss Vandermeer answered. "I heard, while I was downtown this morning, about a boy who was going to drive a dogcart. He came down with measles, and can't be in the parade. So I suggested that Danny's mother get in touch with the boy's family and see if they would let Danny take his place."

The Bobbsey twins thought this sounded very interesting. For a moment Freddie almost wished he could be a dogcart milkman instead of a wind-mill.

The following day was the first day of the Tulpen Feest. The children had no idea that the grownups at Tulip Land Farm were going to take part in the festivities. Therefore, they were amazed when they came down to breakfast to find Uncle Pieter, Aunt Hilda, and Miss Vandermeer in Dutch costumes.

"Oh, Miss Vandermeer, you look so pretty!"

Nan burst out. "I think it would be nice if you'd wear that costume to school sometime."

The teacher laughed gaily. She said that although Nan had been in Tulip Land only four days, she had caught the spirit of the Dutch people.

"But when we get back to Lakeport," the teacher said, "I'm afraid you'd think it strange if I showed up in school in this costume."

All the children wanted to dress up to go to town, but Mrs. Bobbsey pointed out that it would not be possible for Freddie to wear his windmill very long. For this reason, perhaps it would be best for the others to keep their costumes neat and clean for the parade.

"Especially when I have a daughter who falls into canals and a son who rides on windmills," she said, a twinkle in her eye.

The Tulpen Feest holiday had started on Tulip Land Farm. The farm workers already had left for the festival. Presently two cars drew up in front of the door. Uncle Pieter was at the wheel of one, and Miss Vandermeer was driving the other. The Bobbsey family and all the Vandermeers climbed in and started off.

After they had gone over the rustic bridge, which was the only entrance to the island, Mr.

Vandermeer stopped and got out. He walked back, took a key from his pocket, and opened a tiny door in a post by the bridge.

Uncle Pieter reached inside and turned a switch. A moment later, there was a groaning sound. Then, to the Bobbseys' amazement, one end of the bridge began to rise into the air. It swung itself up over the canal and stood almost upright on the island side.

Bert, who was riding with Uncle Pieter, exclaimed, "I didn't know the bridge could rise up."

"I rarely raise it," Uncle Pieter replied. "But today, with no one at home, it's just as well not to have visitors crossing to the house."

"How are you going to get the bridge down again?" Bert questioned.

Uncle Pieter smiled as he drove on. "I think I'll have to ask for a volunteer to go across the canal and send the bridge back over."

"I'll go," Bert offered.

Dirk, who was riding beside Bert, said he would be glad to get the bridge down. At his home in Holland they had exactly the same arrangement and he knew just what to do.

"Only we pull our bridge up every night," the boy said.

"Why?" Bert asked.

Dirk shrugged. There seemed to be no reason except custom. In days gone by in Holland, it had been a means of keeping the cattle from wandering off a farm at night. Since cattle did not like to swim, they did not cross the water.

"You have water fences, don't you?" remarked Flossie, who was on the back seat with Freddie.

"That's right," said Dirk.

Then he and Uncle Pieter laughed, and told the others they were only joking about the bridge. Another turn of the switch, when they got back, and the bridge would come down.

Since the festivities in town would not begin for a while, Uncle Pieter said he would show the visitors a couple of interesting sights.

"First we'll go down to the dock to see if they're loading cheese onto a boat," he said.

The Bobbsey twins once had visited a cheese-making farm, but they had never seen cheese shipped. When they reached the dock, they saw a boat tied up alongside. There was great activity. One man was shouting orders from a truck, another from the boat.

What interested the children most was watching the men pile up the cheeses onto a hand truck. A man standing in the back of a big truck pitched out large, round balls which looked more like pumpkins than like cheeses. A man on the dock caught them and piled them, pyramid style, onto the hand truck. In no time at all he had a high stack. Then, grasping the handle of the cart, he ran up the gangplank onto the boat.

Another man with a hand truck immediately took his place, and the pitching started all over again. How fast they could go!

Bert, who stood watching beside Freddie, chuckled. He remarked that the man in the big truck would make a good baseball pitcher.

"And the other guys are good catchers," Freddie chimed in.

Just as he said this, one of the men missed the catch. The cheese fell to the dock and the boys laughed.

"Hi, son! See if you're a better catcher," the man by the handcart, who seemed to be in charge, called out.

With that, he pitched the cheese directly at Bert. The boy was so startled that he almost missed it, but managed to catch the cheese against his chest like a football. The weight of it, however, forced him off balance, and Bert sat down on the dock with a thud.

It was the cheese man's turn to laugh. "Keep it for a souvenir, son," he said.

"Thanks!" Bert exclaimed. "Golly, it's heavy!" he added.

Uncle Pieter told him that it must weigh close to five pounds, and that it was a pretty nice gift. Bert thought so, too, but wondered how in the world he would ever be able to carry it back to Lakeport.

"I'll give it to you, Uncle Pieter," he said. But the tulip farmer insisted that his wife made all the cheese they could eat and that the Bobbseys should enjoy this. He personally would see about having it shipped to Lakeport.

"Come now," he told the children. "We'll go and watch the man who makes klompen!"

Dirk and Bert put the cheese in the Vander-meer car, then they started back to the main street after Uncle Pieter, who had gone ahead with Flossie and Freddie. Nan and Wanda were a block ahead of them, already watching the elderly shoemaker who was busy making klompen.

The boys had barely started walking up the street to join the others, when suddenly Bert gave a yell.

"Dirk!" he gasped, "I just saw Sam Tomson!" With that, he dashed after the retreating figure.

Dirk remembered the story about his aunt's missing book, and ran after Bert. But Bert went so fast that he could not keep up with him.

Bert Bobbsey disappeared into an alleyway and finally caught up with the man. This time there was no mistake. He was the one who had come to the Bobbsey home and asked where Miss Vandermeer lived.

"Hey!" Bert shouted at him. "Stop!"

Sam Tomson turned around. When he saw Bert, his eyes opened very wide.

"Why, where—?" Suddenly he smiled his crooked smile and asked, as if he had never seen Bert before, "Who are you?"

"You know who I am, all right," Bert replied. "And I know who you are, too. You took our teacher's book and we want it back!"

"I don't know what you're talking about," the man growled. "I never saw you before in my life."

Bert wanted to capture Tomson, but he knew he was no match for a grown man. If the boy expected to get back Miss Vandermeer's valuable book, he would have to get help.

"Police! Police!" he shouted.

CHAPTER XIX

A CASTLE ON TREES

SAM TOMSON was startled by Bert's sudden outburst. Not wanting to be trapped, the man dashed toward the entrance to the alleyway. But Bert got a grip on his coat, and held on with all his might.

"Police!" he yelled again.

The man tried to shove Bert aside, but the boy had a good hold. Sam Tomson decided something must be done in a hurry. Spying a large barrel in a corner, he seized Bert and thrust him into it headfirst. Then the man raced for the street.

Dirk, meanwhile, reached the alley just as Sam Tomson rushed out. Colliding with a thud, they both sprawled on the ground, the man on top of the boy. Desperate, the fugitive hit Dirk on the jaw, stunning the boy momentarily.

Then Sam Tomson jumped up and fled. By the time Dirk started to give chase, Sam Tomson had turned a corner and disappeared.

Poor Bert was having his own troubles. The barrel into which he had been thrown was a flour barrel, practically empty. But the boy's head was covered with the white powder that was left in the bottom.

The barrel had tipped over. Bert backed out of it, sputtering and coughing.

The boy finally got the flour out of his nose and eyes, but he knew there was no use trying to find Sam Tomson now. As he walked down the alley, Bert met Dirk coming to meet him. Dirk stared at his friend in amazement.

"What happened to you?" he asked. "You look as if you had on a white wig."

Bert had been so busy wiping his face that he had completely forgotten about the flour in his hair. As he told Dirk what had happened, he leaned over and shook the flour off as best he could.

"I'm going to get that man yet," he said determinedly.

Dirk told him how he had tried to catch Tomson and failed.

"Which way did he go?" Bert asked excitedly. Dirk pointed. "Maybe it's still not too late to get him!"

The two boys hurried through one street after another but saw no sign of Sam Tomson. When

they finally reached the other children and Uncle
Pieter, Nan looked at her twin's face and hair,
and said:

"Where in the world have you been?"

When Bert told her, Flossie and Freddie giggled. They wanted to go at once and see the flour
barrel, but Uncle Pieter said there were many
other things to do. First of all, he wanted to report to the police that Sam Tomson definitely
was in town.

"You children stay here and watch this klompen maker until I return," he instructed them.

It was fascinating to look at the klompen
maker, who sat in the window of his shop, working cheerfully. He was an elderly man, almost
completely bald. He wore a large shoemaker's
apron, and was seated on a squatty, three-legged
stool, beside a bench. On the bench were all sorts
of tools.

Right now the klompen maker held a wooden
shoe in one hand. With the other, he was chip-
ping out the interior of the shoe with a chisel.

Presently he laid down the tool and smiled at
the children. He motioned for them to come into
his shop.

The Bobbseys were amazed at the place. They
had expected all the shelves to hold klompen.
Instead, they were filled with wooden toys.

The children learned that, years before, the elderly man had worked in a klompen factory in Holland. But since coming to Michigan, he had made only toys.

"During the time of the Tulpen Feest," he said, "I like to show people how klompen are made in Holland."

A clerk, who stood in the aisle, said that the klompen maker was an expert. He could make as many as thirty pairs a day!

"Oh!" said Flossie. "I see why nobody in Holland ever gets wet feet. How many pair of klompen does one child have?"

The man laughed and said he supposed that depended on how much walking a child did, and how fast his little feet grew.

"I have three pairs of shoes," Flossie said. "And pretty soon I'll have to have some more. They're getting tight."

The klompen maker asked her if she thought she would like to wear wooden shoes—he was sure they would not wear out so fast as the leather variety. So Flossie tried on a pair. When the kindly old man saw that they fitted her perfectly, he gave them to her as a souvenir of the Tulpen Feest.

Suddenly Wanda, forgetting she was not in Holland, spoke to the elderly man in Dutch. His eyes brightened, and he began to talk very fast in his native language. Dirk translated for the Bobbseys.

"This man comes from Amsterdam, where we live," he said.

"It's one of the most beautiful places in the world," the klompen maker said. "But what a job it must have been to build that city!"

"What made it so hard?" Freddie spoke up.

The shoemaker said that originally the land had been very soggy and muddy. Before any buildings could be erected, the Dutch people had pounded thousands and thousands of trees down into the mud.

Wanda smiled. "If they hadn't," she said, "the buildings would have slowly sunk into the mud."

"One of the things we learned in school," Dirk said, "is how many trees there are under the Royal Palace in Amsterdam."

"Oh, we saw a model of that in our class exhibit," Nan told the Dutch children. "But I didn't know it was built on top of trees. How many are there under it?"

Together Wanda and Dirk said, "Thirteen thousand, six hundred and fifty-nine!"

"Gee," said Bert, grinning. "That sure is a lot of trees. They must have cut down a whole forest."

"How can you remember the exact number?" Nan asked.

Dirk laughed and said that was easy. The middle numbers were the same as the days in the year, 365. "And you just put a one in front and a nine in back of them," he said.

The klompen maker told his visitors he must get back to work in the window, as several people were waiting to watch the wooden shoes being made. He suggested that the children look around at the toys which he had carved.

"Bert," Freddie called presently, "here's a swell train! Come and look at it."

Bert walked over. The engine and all the cars were made of wood, and were perfect in every detail. As Freddie shoved it along the shelf, the little wheels spun around freely.

In the cab sat the engineer, and there were several passengers inside the coaches. Freddie wanted to buy the train at once, but when Nan picked up the price tag, she said it would take all the money in his piggy bank just to buy the engineer.

"Here's what you ought to have," Flossie called to him.

"What is it?"

"A fire engine!"

Freddie dashed across the shop, and declared

he had never seen a finer toy. Of course he wanted this too, but again the price was more than the children could afford.

"You'd better wait till Daddy comes back," Nan told him. "Anyway," she said, laughing, "maybe tomorrow you'll win the windmill."

Freddie had completely forgotten about the wonderful toy windmill which was to be given as one of the prizes. The little boy immediately decided that this was what he would like most of all.

The children trooped out of the shop just as Uncle Pieter returned. He told Bert that once more the police were starting a hunt for Sam Tomson.

"There must be some good reason why he's staying around here," the tulip farmer remarked with a frown.

"Maybe he's going to take more books," spoke up Flossie, who had heard the conversation.

"I hope not," Mr. Vandermeer said emphatically. "I thought for a time there wasn't much proof that he's a thief, but now I guess there's no doubt about it."

Uncle Pieter thought Sam Tomson never would have run away from Bert, and denied knowing him besides, if he had not been guilty.

"But now let's forget Sam Tomson for a

while," the tulip farmer suggested. "We'd better get up to the main street. The Ice Sweeper is about to put on his show."

"Who is the Ice Sweeper?" Freddie wanted to know.

"Oh, haven't you heard about him?" Uncle Pieter exclaimed. "Well, I'll let you see for yourself!"

CHAPTER XX

THE TULPEN FEEST BEGINS

FREDDIE tried to get Wanda and Dirk to tell him about the Ice Sweeper, but they merely smiled. All the Dutch children said was:

"He'll come along after the street washing."

"Street washing?" Flossie asked, wide-eyed. "What's that?"

Again the children were told to wait and see for themselves. They trotted along beside Uncle Pieter and took a place at the curb. Presently Wanda said:

"Here comes the *Burgemeester!*"

"He's mayor of this town," Uncle Pieter explained. "Today he's dressed like a mayor in old Holland."

The man was attired in a very fine suit of black velvet, with a long, flowing cape to match. He had on knee breeches and wore white stockings. On his polished black shoes were big silver buckles. And on his black, broad-brimmed hat was an even larger silver buckle.

Around the Burgemeester's neck hung a large gold chain from which dangled an enormous key. The small twins asked Uncle Pieter what this was for.

"It's the Key to the City," the tulip farmer replied.

"What does it unlock?" Freddie asked.

Mr. Vandermeer laughed. He said that he had never thought of this. "I suppose it unlocks Tulip Land to all the visitors," he answered.

The Burgemeester stopped walking and began to speak. Although there was not a leaf or a paper to be seen in the street, he declared that, to carry out an old custom, the place must be washed clean before the festivities could begin.

At once several men, wearing Dutch costumes and carrying buckets of water and mops, came into the street. As they started to scrub it, people on the sidewalk laughed. The men seemed very clumsy, as if they were not used to such work.

Also, they were having a lot of fun among themselves. They sloshed water around, getting one another wet. It reminded Nan of one time when she had gone to the circus and had seen some clowns pretending to be working hard, but actually only putting on an act.

One of the men, spying the two sets of twins standing side by side, came up to the Bobbseys.

"Don't you think we've worked long enough?" he asked, grinning. He took Nan by the hand and led her into the street. "I dare you to find any dirt here."

Nan laughed. She said she wished the streets in Lakeport, where she came from, were as clean as this one.

"Then maybe you'd better take this home with you," the man said, a twinkle in his eyes. Suddenly he thrust the bucket and mop into Nan's arms and scooted away.

Nan Bobbsey felt a little foolish, but she knew it was all in fun. People around her began to clap. One lady in a Dutch costume said the little girl was now entitled to the Key to the City, so the Burgemeester hung it around her neck.

He let Nan wear the Key to the City for a few minutes, until the rest of the bucket brigade left the street. As she handed it back to him, Uncle Pieter called out:

"Here comes the Ice Sweeper!"

Down the street came a man on roller skates. He wore baggy breeches and a heavy coat. A fur cap was pulled down over his eyes and a scarf was wound around his neck. In his hand he carried the largest broom the Bobbsey twins had ever seen. As the man skated from one curb to the other, he made great, sweeping motions with the big broom, smiling broadly at the crowd.

"What's he doing that for?" Freddie asked Wanda.

The Dutch girl explained that during the winter everyone in Holland skates on the canals to get from place to place. In order to keep the ice free from slush, men spend all day just sweeping the ice clean.

"I suppose this man is on roller skates," Wanda said. "I've never seen any before; just pictures of them."

Freddie said roller skating was easier than ice skating. "You don't fall down so much," he told her.

Now that the street was clean and ready for festivities, the Burgemeester declared the Tulpen Feest was about to begin.

At once a band started to play. Girls in gay costumes and klompen took their places in the street and began to dance. With hands on their hips and elbows thrust forward, they kept time to the music with a shuffling step and rhythmical kick. Presently the music speeded up. Round and round the dancers went, very fast.

"Golly, how did they ever learn that?" Bert remarked to Dirk. "Can you do it?"

Dirk grinned, saying he was not much of a dancer either in regular shoes or in wooden shoes.

But Wanda was an excellent dancer. He smiled at his sister and said something to her in Dutch.

Turning to Nan, Wanda said that Dirk was telling her she ought to be out there dancing, because she had learned every one of these Dutch dances in school.

"But I wasn't invited," Wanda said, blushing.

Unknown to her, Miss Vandermeer had come up and was standing directly behind the children. Overhearing the remark, she suggested that in the Children's Parade the following day, Wanda and Dirk do a klompen dance together.

"Oh, will it be all right?" Wanda asked, her eyes sparkling.

But the same look did not come into Dirk's face. He told his aunt that he did not want to make a show of himself. He was out of practice.

The teacher laughed. "You sound like a little old man," she said. "Tonight we'll dance at home, and I'll see how bad you are."

After several more dances, the girls left the street. There was a *rat-a-tat-tat* on a drum, then the band started to play a march. The older people who were in costume swarmed into the street and marched along.

"Where are they going?" Flossie turned to ask Miss Vandermeer, but she was gone.

A moment later Flossie spied her in the parade with Uncle Pieter and Aunt Hilda. The children waved to them.

Mrs. Bobbsey, who had come up to the twins, answered Flossie's question. Everyone was headed for the park, where there would be more klompen dancing and music.

"But I think you children have had enough celebration for one day," she said, looking directly at Freddie and Flossie. "We'll take one of the cars and drive back to the farm."

Dirk and Wanda decided to go along with the Bobbseys. As they all walked down a side street, whom should they see but Danny Rugg. He was standing beside a dog-drawn milk cart. The dog was lying in the street.

"Oh, what's the matter with him?" Flossie exclaimed.

All the children rushed ahead to see what had happened. As they reached Danny's side, the big dog arose.

"Go on, you lazy hound!" Danny yelled at the dog. "If you don't, I'll whip you!"

When the dog did not move, Danny slapped him hard.

"Stop that, Danny!" Nan cried out.

The boy turned around and glared at the children from Lakeport. He had not seen them coming down the street.

"You here again?" he asked sullenly. "Well, keep going. I don't need any of your advice!"

"You leave that dog alone!" Bert ordered.

Danny already was angry. He had been trying for fifteen minutes to get the dog to go where he wanted him to. The boy had come out to practice for the Children's Parade, hoping to win a prize. But the dog did not like Danny, and refused to obey.

Danny became very much embarrassed. He did not want the Bobbseys to know that he could not make the dog mind him.

"Giddap there, Major!" he ordered.

The dog turned his head toward Nan Bobbsey and looked pleadingly at her. The girl felt very sorry for him.

"Maybe the dog's tired," she said to Danny. "Why don't you let him go home?"

"I told you to keep out of this!" Danny shouted.

With that he kicked Major on the leg. There was a shrill yelp and, like a flash, the dog raced down the street. The sudden jerk loosened the harness, and the milk cart turned over with a clatter. The dog freed himself and bounded off.

"Oh, he'll run away, and then I can't be in the parade!" Danny wailed.

CHAPTER XXI

A LOCKED BRIDGE

EVERYTHING had happened so quickly that the children simply stood and stared. Then they all started running after the dog.

Bert outdistanced the others. But Major had a head start and was a fast runner.

"Get him, Bert!" Danny kept yelling. He was dropping behind.

"Get him yourself!" cried Freddie, puffing.

Nan suddenly stopped running. Knowing she never could catch the dog, she decided to go back and pick up the cart and milk cans.

"Come on, Flossie and Freddie," she called.

They turned back, although Freddie would have preferred chasing the dog. The children found Mrs. Bobbsey had reached the cart and was righting it and putting the cans back in it.

"Danny's awful mean," Flossie declared. "I don't think he ought to have that nice dog in the parade."

"I ought to have him," Freddie said, then suddenly remembered his windmill suit.

It was nearly ten minutes before Bert and Danny returned with the dog. To the others' amazement it was not Danny but Bert who was leading the sturdy animal. Every time Danny tried to take him, Major would growl.

"I'll harness him," Bert offered.

After the cart was hooked up again, Danny attempted to drive the dog home. But Major seemed to have made up his mind to do no more hauling for Danny. In the end, all the Bobbseys and the Vandermeer children walked the three blocks to the house where the dog lived.

"Tell the man I'll come for Major tomorrow," Danny directed Bert.

"Tell him yourself," Freddie piped up a second time.

At this moment the dog's owner opened the door, and the Bobbseys walked off, leaving Danny to take care of matters as best he could.

"I wonder if he'll be in the parade tomorrow," Nan remarked, as they headed for the car.

"I'll bet the dog won't go with him," said Bert.

Mrs. Bobbsey drove the children back to Tulip Land Farm. As they came through the last field of tulips to the canal, she jammed on the brakes.

They had all forgotten that the bridge to the island was still up!

Bert and Dirk jumped out of the car. "I'll put it down," Dirk offered.

He went to the post at the side of the bridge and tried to open the little door. It was locked.

"I guess Uncle Pieter has the key in his pocket," the Dutch boy remarked. "I'll wade across and see if the box on the other side is unlocked."

But that box was locked too.

"I'll come over," Bert said. "Let's climb up on the bridge and see if we can push it down."

The water was up over their knees, and Mrs. Bobbsey sighed as she thought of more soiled clothes for her family. The children had very few clean ones left!

The boys climbed the upright bridge and shook it with full force, but the bridge would not come down one inch.

"I should have told Mr. Vandermeer we were going home early," Mrs. Bobbsey said, with a sigh. "Well, I guess we'll have to leave the car here and walk the rest of the way." Then she smiled. "Maybe we can save two sets of clothes, at least. Dirk and Bert, suppose you take Freddie and Flossie pickaback across the canal. The rest of us will just have to wade across and get wet."

The small twins thought this was lots of fun, and liked it even better when they were carried all the rest of the way to the farmhouse.

Since the Vandermeers were going to stay in town for the evening, Mrs. Bobbsey and the girls cooked supper. Wanda thought it would be nice to have a United States supper for a change, and asked what the Bobbseys usually ate.

"We don't have supper," Flossie spoke up. "We have dinner, when my daddy comes home."

The twins' mother said she would see what she could find in the icebox to make a United States dinner. When she opened it, Mrs. Bobbsey smiled. Aunt Hilda had left everything prepared!

"Oh, turkey!" Wanda cried. "I love cold turkey."

"I guess that's a favorite dish in every country," Mrs. Bobbsey said. "But, you know, turkeys were discovered in this country."

After dinner she suggested that the small twins go to bed at once. They promised that as soon as they had taken one last look at their parade costumes they would both get ready for bed.

The little twins went upstairs. Presently there was a loud wail from Freddie.

"It's gone!" he cried out.

Flossie rushed into his room, and asked what was gone.

"My suit! My windmill suit!" he said, a sob in his voice.

Nan and her mother went upstairs. Freddie was right. Although they searched the house thoroughly, the costume could not be found. Freddie tried not to cry, but it was hard. He made all sorts of wild guesses as to where the windmill suit had gone, even to blaming Danny Rugg!

"Now, Freddie," his mother said soothingly, "I'm inclined to believe Mrs. Vandermeer put it in some safe place that we haven't thought of. As soon as she comes home, I'll ask her."

It took Freddie a long time to get to sleep, however. The first thing next morning, he knocked on the door of the room Mrs. Bobbsey shared with Miss Vandermeer.

"Come in," said a sleepy voice.

Freddie opened the door. He could hardly believe his eyes. In the center of the room stood the windmill suit!

"You found it!" he shouted joyfully.

"Sh-h!" his mother warned. "Don't awaken Miss Vandermeer."

"I'm awake," the teacher said, turning to face the little boy. "Good morning, Freddie."

"Good morning. Wh—where was my windmill suit?" he asked.

"I'm sorry you were worried about it," Miss Vandermeer said. "I laid the costume on one of the unused beds here, so nothing would happen to it."

Freddie laughed. No one had thought of opening the panels that closed off the wall beds, to look for the suit!

"I wish everybody'd get up," the little boy said. "We have to go to the parade."

Freddie had his wish. Soon all the family gathered at the breakfast table. The children had put on bathrobes, as they would wait until the last minute before donning their costumes.

"Freddie, you put on your regular clothes," his mother said, as soon as he finished his breakfast. "You can slip your costume over them just before the parade starts. And don't ruin your suit!" she cautioned him.

An hour later the children gathered in the living room for inspection. There was a last-minute button to be changed for Flossie, and a switch of caps to be made for Nan.

Uncle Pieter walked in and declared that

every one of the children should receive a prize. Dirk was very handsome in his best suit. Rosy-cheeked Wanda looked unusually pretty in a rose cotton with a blue scarf, and a large, matching Dutch hat with its broad brim turned up.

"Nan, you look very sweet," Aunt Hilda remarked. "And I must say I could almost believe you came right from Holland!"

Nan blushed happily until her cheeks were as pink as Wanda's. "I'm glad you like me in Wanda's dress," she said, adjusting the Dutch lace cap with its turned-back corners.

Flossie as a Dutch doll practiced her jerky walk up and down the room.

"You're perfect," Bert declared.

He himself stood by the door in his Dutch fisherman's clothes. Uncle Pieter had lent him a new clay pipe, and the boy was trying to hold it in his mouth the way he had seen the men do. Over his shoulder he carried a brand-new fish net.

"All ready?" Uncle Pieter asked. "We're taking two cars again."

In all the excitement the children had forgotten to ask about the bridge. Mr. Vandermeer said the key had indeed been in his pocket, and he was sorry his guests had had to wade through the canal.

"Today I'll hide the key, and the first one home can lower the bridge," he said.

Freddie decided at once that he would like to be the first one home, and lower the bridge. Being a bridge tender might be fun even when he was grown up. Yes, he guessed he would raise and lower bridges for a living.

But for the present he had a job to do. The little boy did not want anyone else to hold his windmill suit. He sat on the edge of the rear seat in Uncle Pieter's car, trying to balance the windmill on his lap.

All went well until they reached town. Then Uncle Pieter stopped rather suddenly. Freddie and the windmill toppled to the floor!

CHAPTER XXII

THE PIED PIPER

"OH! OH!" Freddie cried out.

The little boy, falling on top of the windmill suit, scratched his face on the shingles. His upper lip pressed hard against his teeth, causing it to bleed.

But Freddie paid no attention to this. As Nan helped him back onto the seat, and wiped his mouth with a clean handkerchief, he turned the windmill over. Two of the shingles had snapped off!

"Don't cry," Nan said, seeing her small brother's eyes fill with tears. "We'll fix it."

Just how she was going to do this, Nan did not know. Freddie did not, either.

"They're broke, and we didn't bring any hammer and nails," he said.

Uncle Pieter hoped the damage was not serious. Drawing up to the side of the road, he stopped the car and looked at the costume. It certainly was in need of repair. The broken shingles left a gap in the tower of the windmill.

"We'll fix that up in a jiffy," the farmer declared reassuringly.

He stepped from the car and unlocked the trunk compartment. Taking out his tool box, the man searched for some tacks.

Freddie had jumped out, too, and was looking on hopefully. He chuckled as Uncle Pieter found the needed tacks.

"Now let's have the windmill suit, little man," he said. "We'll put those broken shingles back right away."

Freddie lifted the suit out of the car and stood it up on the grass alongside the road. Uncle Pieter told him to steady it, while he tacked the shingles on. Within five minutes, the suit was as good as new again. Freddie was happy.

Flossie, who had been leaning out the window watching, said, "Uncle Pieter, did you take those tacks out of your tires?" She once had heard her father say something about tires picking up tacks in the road.

The man laughed. "No, little lady," he answered, "and please don't suggest a flat tire now. We want to get to the parade!"

He started the car once more, and finally they

reached the town where the Children's Parade was to be held. Many boys and girls already were lined up on the main street.

"Oh, it's be-yoot-i-ful!" Flossie exclaimed.

She and the other Bobbseys had seen several parades, but none more colorful or attractive than this one. The younger children looked very cunning in their Dutch costumes, and most of them wore wooden shoes.

Uncle Pieter inquired of a policeman where the children from Tulip Land Farm should go. He was told that the paraders were being arranged according to height.

"I'm glad I am as tall as you, Nan," Wanda said, smiling. "I'll march alongside of you."

"Oh, aren't you and Dirk going to dance in the parade?" Nan asked her.

Wanda was not sure. She and her brother had practiced the evening before, at Miss Vandermeer's request. It had been decided that if there were music, the two children would do a little dance as they passed the judges.

The girls spoke to a man in charge of the parade. He said it would be all right for both Dirk and Bert to march with the girls. There was not enough difference in their height to separate them.

"Will there be music?" Nan asked him.

"Yes, indeed. But not the kind you're thinking of." He smiled mysteriously and walked off.

The girls went to locate their brothers. Uncle Pieter helped Freddie and Flossie find their places in the line of march.

Freddie was rather hot under his windmill suit, so he decided to leave it off until the last moment. Many of the children came up to admire his unusual costume, and the small twin had to put it on several times to show them how it looked.

"It's swell," said one little boy. "Let me try it on."

Freddie was fearful that something more would happen to his costume, and did not want to lend it. But he also thought that, since he was only a visitor to Tulip Land, perhaps he should not refuse to let the boy try on the costume.

Uncle Pieter saved the situation for him. "I am afraid it would be too small for you," he said to the other lad. "It would be too bad if you got the windmill on and couldn't get it off!"

The boy laughed and said that Mr. Vandermeer was right.

Presently Flossie called out, "Here comes Danny Rugg!"

Danny was walking up a side street with the dogcart. He was having a great deal of trouble with Major. But near him was the dog's owner, the man whose son had the measles and could not be in the parade. Whenever Major got balky, the man would call out for him to behave. Then the dog would trot along a few feet more.

"Do you s'pose the man will have to march in the parade with Danny?" Flossie asked her twin.

"I bet they won't let him," Freddie replied.

Uncle Pieter remarked that, unless the man walked along near Danny, the dog might become unruly. He might even harm some of the children if he made a mad dash through the crowd dragging the cart behind him.

When Danny arrived on the main street, he became the center of attraction. The boy liked this, and at once began to show off.

"Whoa, Major!" Danny shouted at the dog.

But Major did not halt. Danny grinned at the children around and tried again. When the dog did not obey, he said:

"Major's smart. He knows just where to go."

The dog's owner, walking near him, helped to steer Major and the cart along the side of the main street until they reached the section where Danny was to get in line. The boy kept giving orders to Major, and actually did fool many of the children into thinking the animal was obey-

ing him. As he passed one group, Danny said:
"I'm going to win the windmill prize!"

"Oh, is that so?" a boy about his own age spoke
up. "Don't be too sure. I think I will." He wore
dark-red balloon trousers, yellow shirt, and a
dark-red cap, like a Dutch farm boy. He was
leading a young calf.

While this conversation was going on, Bert
had been watching a man on a bicycle. The man
had been riding back and forth looking in the
shopwindows, and paying little attention to the
children who were in the parade. The man wore
a Dutch costume, and around his neck was a scarf
which he had pulled up so that it almost covered
his chin.

The third time Bert caught a glimpse of him he
was sure that he had seen the man somewhere
before. He tried to think where it was. Perhaps
the bicycle rider was one of Uncle Pieter's work-
men.

"I wonder if he has something to do with the
parade," Bert mused.

He thought no more about him, because at that
moment he heard music. It sounded like a flute.
Someone called out that the children were to get
in line.

"Oh, look!" exclaimed Flossie Bobbsey, who
was near the head of the parade with her twin.

From one of the buildings appeared a Pied Piper. Only he looked a little different from pictures of the Pied Piper of Hamelin which the Bobbseys had seen. Suddenly Freddie realized what the difference was.

"He's a Dutch Pied Piper!" he told his sister.

The tall, slender young man took his place at the head of the parade, and began to play on his flute. As he started walking, the children followed, keeping time to the music. Flossie thought she had never done anything more exciting in all her life.

All the children around Flossie and Freddie were smiling. They were very friendly, and talked to the Bobbseys as they marched along.

Everything went all right for a little while, until suddenly Freddie began to have trouble with his windmill suit. First, someone bumped into him accidentally, and shoved it sideways. The little window through which Freddie was looking was pushed away from his eyes. The small boy stumbled and fell. The marcher behind him ran *plunk* into him. He fell, too.

A whistle blew. The Pied Piper stopped playing, and all the marchers halted.

A man ran out from the sidewalk and helped to pick up Freddie. He adjusted the windmill again on top of the little boy's head, and warned the children around him to be careful not to bump into the little walking windmill.

But soon there was more trouble. Freddie decided to twirl the wings of his windmill. As he reached up for the little knob, he again knocked his suit sideways. Since he could not see where he was going, he stopped walking.

This time, three children bumped into him, almost knocking him over. Freddie was on the verge of tears. He was fearful that he might be put out of the parade before the judges had a chance to see him.

"Flossie," he asked, "can't you keep people away from me?"

Flossie, who was walking along jerkily like a real Dutch doll, said she did not see how she could do this and still be a Dutch doll.

"Walk close to me," she suggested. "Then nobody will bump you."

Freddie took his twin's advice, and after that everything went all right. A few minutes later, the Pied Piper turned around to the boys and girls and said:

"Look your best, *jongens en meisjes*. The judges are just ahead."

CHAPTER XXIII

THE DANCERS' REWARD

THE PIED PIPER played especially well as he passed the judges. Then he scooted back to the next section of the parade to lead the older children.

In the meantime, the small children, in their pretty Dutch costumes, stood up straight and marched proudly past the judges. Not one single thing went wrong. The men and women on the reviewing stand clapped and laughed, as well as those along the sidewalks.

"That little Dutch doll is perfect," one bystander said to her husband.

The man chuckled. "That little fellow pretending to be a windmill takes my eye," he said.

Freddie was twirling the wings of his windmill with the little gadget inside the suit. The wings were working perfectly now, and the judges smiled approvingly.

The children walked another block, then turned down a side street. They were told to wait there until all the parade had passed the judges' stand.

"Do you think it would be all right for me to take my suit off now?" Freddie asked his twin. Being a warm May day, it was so hot and stuffy under his costume that he was very uncomfortable.

"I guess so," Flossie replied. "I'll help you put it on again if you have to."

She lifted off the windmill suit. The little boy took a deep breath of fresh air. Then he said:

"What do you s'pose Bert and Nan are doing?"

He wished he might run back and see his brother and sister marching along, but a man who was standing with the children insisted that he stay where he was. Another little boy in the crowd wanted to know why.

"Maybe some of you will be asked to go back and let the judges look at you again," the man explained. "If you wander off, you may lose your chance to win a prize."

This remark made Flossie recall the lovely princess doll she had seen in the department-store window. How she would love to own it! Did she really look like it in her Dutch costume, as some of the grownups had said?

Suddenly the twins could hear the Pied Piper playing his flute again. The second group of pa raders was now marching past the judges' stand.

At that very moment Dirk and Wanda were doing their klompen dance. The judges leaned forward, very much interested in the steps. As the two children locked arms and whirled around, one woman said:

"I've never seen that dance before. Isn't it unusual? I wonder where they learned it?"

"I saw that danced in Holland when I was there last year," one of the men spoke up. "Those children must be the ones from Holland who are visiting the Vandermeers."

"They're adorable," said another woman judge.

"I vote they get a prize." said one of the men, smiling. The other judges bobbed their heads in agreement.

Directly behind Wanda and Dirk marched the older Bobbsey twins. They were so busy watching the Vandermeer children that they forgot to look at the judges. Suddenly Bert and Nan realized they had gone past them. The twins were having a wonderful time, with no thought of winning prizes, anyway. There were many girls of Nan's age whose costumes were as pretty as her own, and the boys of Bert's age certainly looked very well.

"I think the boy with the calf ought to get a

prize," Nan said to Bert as the paraders were ushered down another side street next to the one on which the small twins were waiting.

Bert grinned. "That sure would make Danny sore," he said.

At this very moment Danny, who was the last in line, was coming past the reviewing stand. He was leading the dog, who was behaving quite well. Nevertheless, his owner, on the sidewalk near by, was keeping an eye on both Danny and Major.

Suddenly Danny decided to put on a show. He wanted to prove to the judges that now he had complete control of the dog and could make him go very fast. The boy gave Major a sudden yank and started to run.

Major did not want to run. With a growl he jerked himself loose from Danny and pulled back. The sudden movement made the boy lose his balance. Right in front of the judges' stand he fell flat on his face!

Danny was very much embarrassed, and Major's owner was angry. He did not like the way Danny had treated the dog from the beginning, but out of friendship for Miss Vandermeer he had allowed the boy to borrow Major and the dogcart.

Now the man hurried into the street and said

he would take charge. Danny began to whine that he had a right to finish the parade, but the dog's owner refused to let him touch Major. As a matter of fact, Major refused too. Each time Danny tried to take hold of him, he growled angrily. Finally, there was nothing for Danny to do but leave the parade.

After the paraders had waited a few minutes, it was announced that they were to go to the park. The prizes had been taken there and would be awarded in a few minutes.

The Pied Piper started playing again. He led the small children to the park, and the older ones fell in line behind them. Just as they were nearing it, Bert spied the bicycle rider whom he had seen before and thought he knew.

Bert wished he could remember who the man was. As he watched intently, the rider got off his bicycle and laid it on the grass. Then he became lost to Bert's view as he mingled with the grownups and children.

The Pied Piper mounted a little platform and began to play his lovely music again. The paraders stood around expectantly. It seemed as if the judges were very slow in arriving. But finally the men and women reached the park and took their places on chairs just back of the Pied Piper.

He stopped playing, and one of the men arose.

"Boys and girls," he said, "this is a beautiful day, and also one of the happiest of my life. But it also is one of the hardest. You children are the ones who have made it hard for me."

The listening children wondered why. In a moment he explained.

"Each one of you looks so fine that the committee thinks every boy and girl should have a prize. Of course, this is not possible.

"In fact," he added, chuckling, "there wouldn't have been any prizes at all, if it hadn't been for our good friend Mrs. Volen. As you have heard, her home contains many beautiful articles. She wants others to share some of her possessions, and decided that the Tulpen Feest would be the appropriate time.

"Today we shall award the lovely toys she has given, and tomorrow your fathers and mothers and aunts and uncles will have a chance to win the grownups' prizes. The diamond-studded, golden klompen are, of course, the grand prize."

The man stopped speaking a moment. Freddie, who had climbed back into his windmill suit, thought it was too bad the man had to make such a long speech. Why didn't he give out the children's prizes?

The judge started speaking again. "But even
if you children could win the jeweled klompen,
I'm sure you prefer the dolls and windmills."

"You bet I do!" Freddie called out.

"Sh!" Flossie warned him.

But the man did not seem to mind Freddie's
interruption. He said, pointing toward the twin,
"There's a little man after my own heart."

He now mentioned the list of children's prizes.
Then he said that the judges had made their de-
cisions, and that Mrs. Volen would announce the
winners. There was complete silence in the park
as the old lady arose and came forward.

"Our Tulpen Feest has attracted men and
women from many parts of the country," she
said, "but we rarely have children visit us, because they are busy at school in their own towns.
But this week we are fortunate in having some
unusual child visitors with us. We are not giving
prizes to all of them, but we do want the rest of
you to meet them.

"Visiting us, and in our parade today, are two
sets of twins—the Bobbseys from Lakeport. Will
they please come forward?"

As the twins walked up on the platform, Mrs.
Volen introduced each of them by name, and
everyone clapped. It did not occur to Bert and
Nan to speak, but Flossie and Freddie, excited,

said at the same time, "We like being twins."

The crowd laughed. Then Mrs. Volen went on to say that a boy and his sister were visiting from Holland. She asked Dirk and Wanda also to step to the platform and take a bow.

"These children did a very pretty little dance in the parade," Mrs. Volen said. "Most of you could not see it, so I'm going to ask Dirk and Wanda to dance for you now. Then we shall present them with a prize which is distinctly American, and I hope they will enjoy playing with it after they return to Holland."

The Pied Piper played his flute, and the two Dutch children danced even better than they had in the parade. As they finished, Mrs. Volen handed them a model American plane piloted by Santa Claus as American children know him.

As everyone applauded, Wanda said, "Oh, thank you, thank you so much," and Dirk added with a smile, "I'm so glad to have an American airplane and be able to show my friends at home what your Santa Claus looks like."

Mrs. Volen smiled. As the clapping stopped, she started to speak again. But before she could say anything, an elderly man came running from behind the judges' stand. He cried out excitedly:

"The golden klompen! The diamond-studded klompen! They've been stolen!"

CHAPTER XXIV

IN THE NET

THE disturbing news ran through the crowd. The grand prize had been stolen!

"How did it happen?" Mrs. Volen asked excitedly.

The man who had run over to make the announcement began to talk very fast. By mistake, someone on the committee had brought the diamond-studded golden klompen to the park with the children's prizes. A few moments before, the jeweled shoes had been on the stand. Now they were gone.

"This is dreadful," Mrs. Volen said. "We'd better call the police."

Many of the children waiting to hear which of them were to receive prizes stared in amazement. They began to talk excitedly.

The only one who made a sudden move was Bert Bobbsey. A thought had come to him.

The man in Dutch costume, riding a bicycle! *He was Sam Tomson!*

Nan, noticing her brother make a wild dash through the paraders, ran after her twin. She tried to catch up to him, but the boy was fairly flying through the park. In the distance was the man on the bicycle. He was pedaling rapidly.

When Bert came to the street he could not see the rider. But as the boy reached a corner, he spied the man and darted after him.

Bert Bobbsey had never run faster in his life. In school games he was known as a good runner, and in races he usually came in first. But he bettered even that speed as he went headlong down the street.

The man on the bicycle, although riding at a good clip, was not aware that anyone was chasing him. Bert did not dare call for help, since he did not want to make another mistake such as he had in Lakeport, when he went after the wrong man.

The cyclist turned another corner. Bert almost lost him. Then the boy found him once more. Now he was actually gaining on the man.

Far behind Bert came Nan. She could not possibly keep up with her twin, but she was calling to him. Bert glanced over his shoulder.

"I might need Nan's help," he thought. "I'd better let her know where I'm going." But he did not dare stop. What could he do?

Suddenly Bert thought of a game he and his twin often played. Around his shoulders was the new fish net that went with his costume. A paper tag was still tied to one corner. Quickly Bert tore off bits of it. As he turned down the side street, he left a trail of paper.

In a few minutes Nan reached the spot and looked around for Bert. Then she spied the bits of paper on the clean-swept street. Perhaps her twin had dropped them! She dashed off in the direction he had taken.

By this time, Bert was very close to the man on the bicycle. Suddenly the rider turned around. There was no doubt of it. He was Sam Tomson!

Seeing the boy in pursuit, Sam Tomson put on a burst of speed. In a moment he was well ahead again and disappeared around another corner.

Apparently the man then changed his mind about where he was going. As Bert rounded the corner, there stood the bicycle, propped up against a building. Sam Tomson himself was out of sight!

Bert, panting, stood still, regaining his breath. Where had the man gone? He concluded that the thief must have darted down an alleyway which led to the lake front.

Quickly tearing off two more pieces of paper, Bert dropped one on the street and put the other just inside the alleyway. Nan was not in sight, but Bert was sure she would come along soon.

He dashed down the alleyway to a dock. Still he could not see Sam Tomson. But as the boy looked around, he heard a slight rustling sound. Walking toward it, he spied the suspected thief hiding behind a boat which had been hauled up on the dock for repair.

"I've caught you!" Bert exclaimed.

"Caught me?" Sam Tomson asked. "What are you talking about?"

"You stole the golden klompen!" Bert said.

"You're crazy!" Sam Tomson shouted.

Bert wished Nan would come. Perhaps together they could hold Sam Tomson until help might arrive. But nobody was in sight. Everyone was uptown at the Tulpen Feest.

He was afraid that if he shouted for aid the man might dash off again. The best thing to do was to try to keep him there until Bert could somehow get help.

"You took our teacher's book!" he said. "When are you going to give that back?"

Sam Tomson did not answer. Instead, he came from behind the boat and walked menacingly toward the boy. Bert stood his ground. Then he saw the man double his fists. As he aimed a blow, Bert ducked.

At this very second, Nan Bobbsey appeared at the end of the alleyway. Seeing her brother attacked by Sam Tomson, she ran to Bert's aid. When Tomson spied her, he let out a yelp of surprise and turned to push Nan out of the way. But as he raised his hand, Bert grasped it from behind and spun the man around so hard that he lost his balance and fell on his back.

The thief knew that he was losing time. He scrambled to his feet and tried to dash off the dock, but Bert barred his way. Suddenly, in desperation, Sam Tomson ran to the water's edge and dived into the lake.

"Oh, Bert, we've lost him!" Nan said woefully, looking at the ripples in the water.

"No, we haven't," her twin answered, and promptly kicked off his shoes and dived in.

Bert rose to the surface, and looked around for Sam Tomson. He could not see him anywhere in the water.

Nan, at the edge of the dock, was looking around, too, but Sam Tomson had disappeared completely. Nan shuddered. Even though the man might be a thief, she did not want anything dreadful to happen to him.

Bert, too, was beginning to wonder if Sam Tomson had hit his head when he dived. The water was not very deep. Bert himself had made a shallow dive. Now he went under again and peered through the dim water, but did not see Sam Tomson.

Rising to the surface once more, Bert suddenly had an idea. He looked under the dock. There was Sam Tomson clinging to one of the posts!

He ordered Bert away, growling that if the boy came near him he would be sorry. Bert knew the man meant it.

Looking up, he said to Nan, "He's under there. You go for help."

As Nan ran off to hunt for a policeman, Bert watched Sam Tomson. The boy figured that the best thing to do was to follow him if he should leave the spot.

Suddenly Nan's voice came to their ears. She was crying, "Police! Police!" loudly.

This made Sam Tomson decide to move. Sinking beneath the surface, the man disappeared. Bert dived under and looked around. He could just see him swimming underwater toward shore.

The suspected thief reached it and quickly climbed up on the bank. Bert was right after him. As the man staggered up the embankment, Bert came out of the water, took the fish net from around his neck, and threw it.

The net landed neatly over Sam Tomson's head.

CHAPTER XXV

THE GOLDEN BOBBSEY

AS THE fish net came down over Sam Tomson, the man stumbled and fell. Before he could get up, Bert reached his side. Quickly he pulled the ends of the net together and held his prisoner tight.

Sam Tomson looked comical, flopping around inside the net like a big fish. He tried hard to get up. But Bert held him fast.

Just then, running footsteps sounded in the alleyway. A moment later, Nan Bobbsey appeared with a policeman.

"You caught a thief, eh?" the officer said. "Good for you!"

"Get me out of here!" Sam Tomson shouted, still trying to struggle to his feet.

But the officer did not take the net off Sam Tomson at once. The prisoner declared his innocence of any wrongdoing, and said they had no right to treat him this way. He began shouting again.

"Just a minute," the officer said. "The police have been looking for you for several days. You're going to come along with me to head-quarters, and answer a few questions. Will you go without making any trouble, or do you want to stay inside the net awhile?"

It was several minutes before Sam Tomson promised to be good. Then Bert and the police-man removed the net, and Bert put it back around his neck.

"Aren't you going to search Sam Tomson?" Bert questioned the policeman. "I think you might find the jeweled klompen on him!"

Both Nan and the officer looked amazed at Bert's statement. The little girl had told the policeman she was sure the prisoner had stolen Miss Vandermeer's valuable book. But they had no idea he might also be the one who had stolen the golden klompen.

"I'll say I'll search him," the policeman re-plied.

As he looked through the prisoner's pockets, Sam Tomson smiled one of his crooked smiles. There was nothing in his pockets but a little money and a couple of water-soaked letters.

"You see!" he said triumphantly. "Now let me go."

"Wait a minute!" Bert cried out. "I have an

idea. I'll bet I know where Mr. Tomson hid the jeweled klompen."

At this, Sam Tomson became uneasy, and Bert was sure his guess had been right. Diving into the water, the boy swam under the dock to the post where he had found the man hiding a few minutes before.

Bert was right. Lying on top of the post, between two planks, lay the diamond-studded, golden klompen! Bert grabbed them, and swam back to the waiting group. Pulling himself up on shore, he exclaimed:

"I found them!"

His announcement so astonished the others that for a moment the policeman took his eyes from the prisoner. In that instant, Sam Tomson made a dash for freedom.

It did him no good, however. He was quickly caught, and marched to police headquarters. Bert retrieved his shoes and the twins went along. While Bert was in a little room having his clothes dried for him, Nan, at the captain's desk, told all she knew about Sam Tomson.

Upon a careful reading of the water-soaked letters in his pockets, it was revealed that he was using another name in Tulip Land. From the address on the envelope it was also learned where the thief was staying.

The policeman who had brought Tomson in was sent to search the prisoner's bedroom. In it was found a large sum of money as well as a book of names of people to whom he had sold stolen books, including Miss Vandermeer's.

When the policeman returned, Sam Tomson admitted that he was a thief. Up to the time of taking the jeweled klompen, however, he had stolen only rare, valuable books.

"I learned about the one Miss Vandermeer had in Lakeport," he said, "so I went there to take it. Then I heard the Bobbsey twins and their teacher talking at her house one day. She was telling them about this part of Michigan. I thought it might be a good place to come and sell the book, especially during the Tulip Festival."

Sam Tomson said also that when he heard about the prize klompen he had hung around, hoping there might be a chance to steal them. The chance had come when someone had taken them to the park by mistake with the children's prizes.

By this time, Bert's clothes had dried and he came out to the main room. The policeman praised him and Nan highly for capturing the thief, and said they would recover Miss Vandermeer's rare book at once and return it to her.

"We'd better go back to the park now," Nan

told her twin. "I suppose the show is all over, though."

The show had been over for some time, and all the prizes had been given out. Among the proud children who had received prizes were Freddie and Flossie Bobbsey. As Nan and Bert came up to them, Freddie cried out gleefully:

"I got the windmill! It's all mine!"

"Gee, that's swell!" Bert said, and Nan kissed her little brother.

The older twins now noticed that Flossie was hugging a doll tightly. It was the lovely princess doll which the children had seen among the prizes.

"They gave her to me, 'cause they said I look like her," Flossie told them. "Oh, isn't she be-yootiful!"

As Flossie held the doll up, Bert and Nan had to agree that their little sister in her Dutch costume and klompen surely did look like the Dutch princess doll.

"I'm sorry you didn't get a prize, Nan," Flossie spoke up.

"And you, too, Bert," Freddie added.

"I guess we got the best prize of all," Nan said, smiling.

As Dirk and Wanda came up—they had been looking all over for Bert and Nan—the older twins told their exciting story of the capture of Sam Tomson. Dirk and Wanda were amazed. Freddie's and Flossie's eyes fairly popped.

In a few moments, word spread among the crowd that the jeweled klompen had been found by the older Bobbsey twins. The children were made to stand up on the platform, and everyone applauded them.

Even Danny Rugg applauded, though he wished he had been the one to capture the thief.

Nan and Bert were embarrassed by all the attention they were receiving, and wanted to get away as soon as possible. Their mother and the Vandermeers, who also had been looking for them, came up, and said how happy they were about the outcome of the twins' adventure.

Miss Vandermeer put her arms around Nan and Bert. "How can I ever thank you properly?" she asked.

"Promote them," Freddie piped up.

Everyone laughed, and Miss Vandermeer said that the twins were so good in their work that she was sure they would pass anyway.

"No, I'll have to think up something else," she said. "I believe Uncle Pieter will have to help me out."

She would say no more, and the children wondered what she had in mind. They were sure it would be something very nice, whatever it was.

The following day, the children watched the big parade of the grownups. Many beautiful costumes of Holland were displayed, and the judges had just as hard a time awarding the prizes as they had had in the Children's Parade. Everyone was excited when the moment came to award the grand prize. Then shouts of glee arose when the Bobbsey twins and their friends realized that the golden, diamond-studded klompen had been awarded to—Miss Vandermeer!

All the way home the children chattered excitedly, and Miss Vandermeer, delighted with her prize, thanked Nan and Bert once again. "For," she pointed out, "if you hadn't caught the thief, there would have been no golden klompen to win."

When they reached home, Mrs. Bobbsey said they must get ready to fly back to Lakeport.

"I hate to see you go," Wanda said, putting her arms around Nan. "M-maybe I'll never see you again."

"On your way home, maybe you can stop off at Lakeport," Nan said.

"Oh, that will be wonderful!" Wanda cried. "I'll do it."

Dirk and Bert had grown to be good friends, too, and when they heard the suggestion, they thought it was fine. The Dutch children planned to stay in Tulip Land until the end of summer. Then they would come to Lakeport for a visit before returning to Holland.

"We want you to take something with you," Wanda said to Bert and Nan just before bedtime.

She and Dirk looked at each other, then went off mysteriously. Presently they returned and handed a package to each of the twins. Upon opening them, Nan and Bert found two pairs of shiny figure skates.

"You—you're going to give these to us?" Bert exclaimed.

The Dutch children nodded. With a laugh, they explained that, upon leaving home, they had brought their skates, hoping to have a chance to use them in the United States; but now they knew they would be back in their native land long before there was any ice.

"After we heard our aunt say she wanted you to have a special gift," Dirk said, "we asked her if she thought you'd like these."

"Please have fun on them the way we did," Wanda said.

Bert and Nan were thrilled at the gift. They felt it would take them some time to become good figure skaters, but they certainly would practice.

The next morning, Mr. Bobbsey arrived.

When he heard all that had happened in his absence, he laughed and said:

"I had a good trip too, but not nearly so exciting as your adventures here."

When the Bobbsey family was ready to leave the Vandermeer farm, Uncle Pieter came into the house with an exquisite bouquet of yellow tulips. His eyes were twinkling.

"These flowers are for you to take home," he said. "This fall I'll send you a box of bulbs of the same variety."

Mr. and Mrs. Bobbsey thanked their host and hostess warmly for the lovely flowers, as well as for their hospitality. Then Nan said:

"These are the most beautiful tulips on your farm."

"I think they are, too," Uncle Pieter replied. "They are a new variety on which I have been working for some time."

"What is it called?" Freddie spoke up.

"I have named it in honor of your family," the tulip farmer replied. "I'm calling it the 'Golden Bobbsey.'"

"Just like Flossie's curls!" Freddie exclaimed. And when the little girl shook her curls, they did look like yellow tulips swaying in the wind.

THE BOBBSEY TWINS have still more fun and adventures in the next book:

THE BOBBSEY TWINS IN RAINBOW VALLEY

Don't miss this exciting story of how the twins solve the secret of the singing waterfall.